FUN學

美國各學科初級課本

新生入門英語閱讀 二版

③

AMERiCAN
SCHOOL
TEXTBOOK

Reading Key BASIC

作者 ◎ Michael A. Putlack & e-Creative Contents

譯者 ◎ 陸葵珍

MP3

寂天雲 APP

如何下載 MP3 音檔

❶ **寂天雲 APP 聆聽：** 掃描書上 QR Code 下載「寂天雲－英日語學習隨身聽」APP。加入會員後，用 APP 內建掃描器再次掃描書上 QR Code，即可使用 APP 聆聽音檔。

❷ **官網下載音檔：** 請上「寂天閱讀網」（www.icosmos.com.tw），註冊會員／登入後，搜尋本書，進入本書頁面，點選「MP3 下載」下載音檔，存於電腦等其他播放器聆聽使用。

American School Textbook
Reading Key
Basic

The Best Preparation for Building Academic Reading Skills and Vocabulary

The Reading Key series is designed to help students to understand American school textbooks and to develop background knowledge in a wide variety of academic topics. This series also provides learners with the opportunity to enhance their reading comprehension skills and vocabulary.

○ **Reading Key <Basic 1–4>** is a four-book series designed for beginning learners.

○ **Reading Key <Volume 1–3>** is a three-book series designed for beginner to intermediate learners.

○ **Reading Key <Volume 4–6>** is a three-book series designed for intermediate to high-intermediate learners.

○ **Reading Key <Volume 7–9>** is a three-book series designed for high-intermediate learners.

Features

• A wide variety of topics that cover American school subjects
• Intensive practice for reading skill development
• Building vocabulary through school subjects and themed texts
• Graphic organizers for each passage
• Captivating pictures and illustrations related to the topics

Table of Contents

Component

• Workbook

Syllabus Vol. 3

Chapter

1

Social Studies

★

History and Geography

Unit 01

Thanks, Thomas Edison

Reading Focus

- What is an inventor?
- What does an inventor do?
- How do inventors help us?

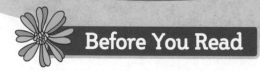

 01

Key Words

Famous Inventions

light bulb

phonograph

motion picture camera

telephone

airplane

Famous Inventors

Thomas Edison

Alexander Graham Bell

Orville and Wilbur Wright
(the Wright brothers)

Power Verbs

turn on
Turn on the light.

turn off
Turn off the light.

be born
He was born in America.

grow up
He grew up in the country.

invent
He invented the light bulb.

Word Families: Adjectives for Invention

Inventor

curious
a curious boy

famous
a famous inventor

Invention

fast
a fast airplane

convenient
a convenient telephone

Thanks, Thomas Edison

We turn on a light when it's dark.
Do you know who made the electric light?
It was Thomas Edison.

Thomas Edison was a famous inventor.
He was born in 1847 in America.
He was a very curious boy.
He always asked questions. "Why?" "Why is that?"
When he grew up, he became an inventor.

▲ Thomas Edison was a famous inventor.

An inventor makes new things.
We call these new things inventions.

Thomas Edison made many inventions.

▲ An inventor makes new things.

He invented the electric light bulb.
Thanks to electric lights, we can see at night.

He invented the phonograph.
Thanks to him, we can listen to music with a stereo.

He invented the motion picture camera.
Thanks to him, we can see movies.

Thomas Edison also invented many other things.
He made more than 1,000 inventions!
His inventions made our lives more convenient.

▲ Thanks to electric lights, we can see at night.

There are many other inventions in the world.
Inventions make our work easier and faster.
Do you know some of them?

▸ The telephone and computer
make our work easier and faster.

Check Understanding

1 **Which type of invention does each picture show?**

 a

 b

_____   _____

2 **What question did Thomas Edison always ask?**
   a Where?   b Why?   c Who?

3 **How does the electric light help us?**
   a We can see at night.   b We can listen to music.
   c We can see movies.

4 **Thomas Edison invited the _____ so we can listen to music with a stereo.**
   a light bulb   b phonograph
   c motion picture camera

   • **Answer the questions below.**

   1 What does an inventor do?
      ⇨ An inventor makes _____ _____.

   2 How did Thomas Edison's inventions help our lives?
      ⇨ His inventions made our lives_____ _____.

Vocabulary and Grammar Builder

A **Look, Read, and Write.**
Look at the pictures. Write the correct words.

> invented   turn on   born   stereo

1

▶ Please _____ the light.

2

▶ Edison was _____ in America.

3

▶ Edison _____ the light bulb.

4

▶ We can listen to music with a _____.

B **Curious or Convenient?**
Draw a circle around the right words and then write the words.

1 Thomas Edison was very _____.
curious   convenient

2 Inventions make our lives more _____.
curious   convenient

3 Inventions make our work _____.
easier   harder

4 Airplanes help people move _____.
slower   faster

Unit 02

The First Man Into Space

Reading Focus

- What is an astronaut?
- What do astronauts do?
- Who was the first person in space?

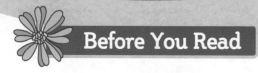

Before You Read

03

Key Words

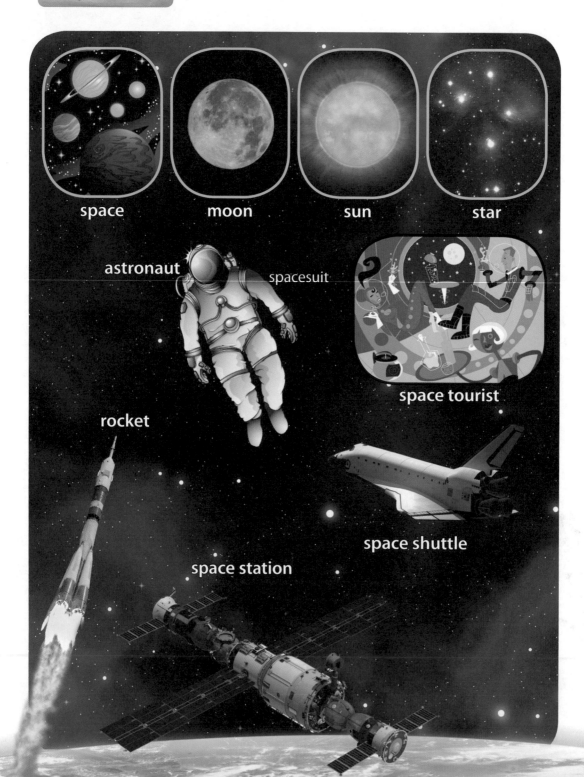

space

moon

sun

star

astronaut

spacesuit

space tourist

rocket

space shuttle

space station

16

Power Verbs

travel into
Astronauts **travel into** space.

explore
Astronauts **explore** the moon.

go into
A rocket **goes into** space.

lift off
A space shuttle **lifts off**.

protect
Spacesuits **protect** astronauts.

travel around
He **traveled around** Earth.

Word Families: The First Human in Space

The First
Into Space

Yuri Gagarin

Neil Armstrong

The First Man Into Space 🎧 04

Do you like traveling to new places?
Where would you like to go?
How about traveling into space?

Some people travel into space.
They are astronauts.
Astronauts explore space and learn about it.

▲ Astronauts explore space and learn about it.

Who was the first human in space?
It was Yuri Gagarin, a Russian astronaut.
He went into space for the first time in 1961.

This is the Kennedy Space Center.
It is in Florida in the USA.
Many astronauts go into space
from the Kennedy Space Center.
Space shuttles lift off from the center.

▲ Kennedy Space Center

Astronauts wear spacesuits.
Their spacesuits protect them in space.

In 1969, American astronauts went to
the moon for the first time.
Neil Armstrong was the first person
to walk on the moon.

▲ Neil Armstrong was the first person to walk on the moon.

Sally Ride was the first American woman in space.

Mae Jemison was the first African-American woman in space.

Dennis Tito was the first space tourist.

He traveled around Earth in 2001.

Check Understanding

1 What does each picture show?

_____   _____

2 Where do astronauts explore?

a space center   b space   c spacesuits

3 What do astronauts wear?

a spacesuits   b space centers   c space shuttles

4 The first person to walk on the moon was _____.

a Neil Armstrong   b Yuri Gagarin   c Sally Ride

• **Answer the questions below.**

1 Who was the first human in space?

⇨ _____ _____ was the first human in space.

2 Where is the Kennedy Space Center?

⇨ It is in _____ in the _____.

A **Look, Read, and Write.**
Look at the pictures. Write the correct words.

| spacesuits | space shuttle | astronauts | explored |

1  ▶ _____
wear spacesuits.

2  ▶ _____
protect astronauts
in space.

3  ▶ Neil Armstrong
_____ the
moon in 1969.

4  ▶ A _____
lifts off.

B **On or Off?**
Draw a circle around the right words and then write the words.

1 Astronauts travel _____ space.
on   into

2 Space shuttles lift _____ from the Kennedy Space Center.
on   off

3 American astronauts went to the moon _____ the first time in 1969.
for   to

4 The first space tourist traveled _____ Earth in 2001.
off   around

03

Storms

Reading Focus

- What is a storm?
- What is a blizzard?
- How can storms hurt people?

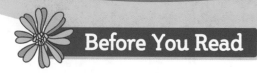
Before You Read

05

Key Words

Storms

thunderstorm

rainstorm

snowstorm

lightning

flood

blizzard

thunder

strong wind

22

Power Verbs

strike
Lightning can **strike** trees.

make a sound
Thunder **makes** a loud **sound**.

bring
Storms can **bring** heavy rain.

cause
Storms can **cause** floods.

overflow
Some rivers **overflow**.

fall
Snow **falls** in the winter.

Word Families: The Adjectives for Storms

dark

dark clouds

loud

loud sounds

strong

strong winds

heavy

heavy rain

harmful

Storms can be harmful.

23

Storms

Look up at the sky.
The clouds are big and dark.
A storm is coming.

Flash! Lightning strikes across the sky.
Boom! Thunder makes a loud sound.
It is a thunderstorm.

Sometimes we have storms.
Storms can be harmful.
Storms can bring strong winds.
Storms can bring heavy rain or snow.

A thunderstorm has thunder, lightning, and heavy rain.
Sometimes lightning strikes trees and tall buildings.
Sometimes heavy rain causes floods.
Rivers and streams overflow.
Some land is covered with water.

06

▲ Storms can bring strong
winds and heavy rain.

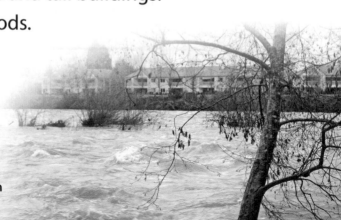

▶ Sometimes heavy rain
causes floods.

When it is cold, a lot of snow may fall.
A big snowstorm is called a blizzard.
A blizzard has strong winds.
In a blizzard, snow falls so heavily
that people can only see white.

▲ blizzard

Check Understanding

1 **Which kind of storm does each picture show?**

a _____

b _____

2 **What does thunder do?**
   a It makes a loud sound.   b It strikes trees.
   c It causes a flood.

3 **What can heavy rain cause?**
   a fast winds   b floods   c blizzards

4 **A big snowstorm is called a _____.**
   a thunderstorm   b rainstorm   c blizzard

• **Answer the questions below.**

1 What does a thunderstorm have?
   ⇨ A thunderstorm has _____, _____,
      and _____ _____.

2 What does a blizzard have?
   ⇨ A blizzard has strong _____ and heavy _____.

25

A **Look, Read, and Write.**
Look at the pictures. Write the correct words.

strike   thunderstorm   blizzard   overflow

1 ▸ A _____ has thunder and lightning.

2 ▸ Rivers and streams _____.

3 ▸ Lightning can _____ trees and buildings.

4 ▸ A _____ is a big snowstorm.

B **Loud or Dark?**
Draw a circle around the right words and then write the words.

1 Thunder makes a _____ sound.
      loud   dark

2 _____ rain can cause a flood.
      Strong   Heavy

3 A blizzard has _____ winds.
      strong   heavy

4 Storms can be _____.
      harmful   dark

Unit **04**

Tornadoes and Hurricanes

Reading Focus

- What is a tornado?
- What is a hurricane?
- How are these storms dangerous?

Key Words

Tornado

funnel-shaped cloud

twister

tornado warning

tornado alarm

tornado shelter

Hurricane

the eye

Power Verbs

rush
People **rush** to shelter.

spin
A tornado **spins** like a top.

lift
A tornado can **lift** many things.

blow away
A tornado can **blow away** a house.

destroy
The hurricane **destroyed** the city.

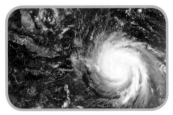

form
A hurricane **forms** on the ocean.

Word Families: The Adjectives for Tornados

 **strange** ➡ The sky looks strange.

 **dangerous** ➡ A hurricane can be dangerous.

 **funnel-shaped** ➡ A tornado has a funnel-shaped cloud.

Tornadoes and Hurricanes

The sky begins to look strange.
The clouds are low and purple.
The wind begins to blow hard.
Suddenly, a loud alarm sounds.
People rush to shelter.
A tornado is coming.

▲ A tornado has a
funnel-shaped cloud.

Big thunderstorms can make a tornado.
It has a funnel-shaped cloud with strong winds.
This funnel-shaped cloud spins like a top.

Tornado winds blow very fast.
A tornado can be very dangerous.

A tornado can lift many things.
It can even lift trucks and blow them away.
It can destroy buildings and kill people.

▲ A tornado can lift many things.

A huge rainstorm is called a hurricane.
A hurricane has very strong winds.
It forms on the ocean.
But hurricanes often move onto land.
Heavy rain falls during a hurricane.
The center of a hurricane is called the eye.

the eye of a hurricane

Check Understanding

1 Which kind of storm does each picture show?

a

b

_____   _____

2 What does a tornado cloud look like?

  a a circle   b a funnel   c an eye

3 A huge rainstorm is called a _____.

  a tornado   b hurricane   c ocean

4 The _____ of a hurricane is the eye.

  a center   b side   c top

• Answer the questions below.

1 Where do people go during a tornado?
⇨ People go to _____.

2 What does a hurricane have?
⇨ A hurricane has very strong _____ and heavy _____.

31

A **Look, Read, and Write.**
Look at the pictures. Write the correct words.

| spins | eye | blow away | rush |

 **1** ▶ A tornado _____ like a top.

 **2** ▶ People _____ to shelter.

 **3** ▶ A tornado can _____ a house.

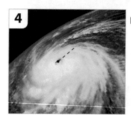 **4** ▶ The center of a hurricane is called the _____.

B **Strange or Dangerous?**
Draw a circle around the right words and then write the words.

   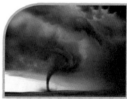

1 The sky begins to look _____.
strange   dangerous

2 A hurricane can be very _____.
safe   dangerous

3 A tornado has a _____ cloud.
funnel-shaped   loud

4 When a tornado is coming, the wind begins to blow _____.
soft   hard

A Look at the pictures. Write the correct words.

> forms   astronauts   invented   thunderstorm

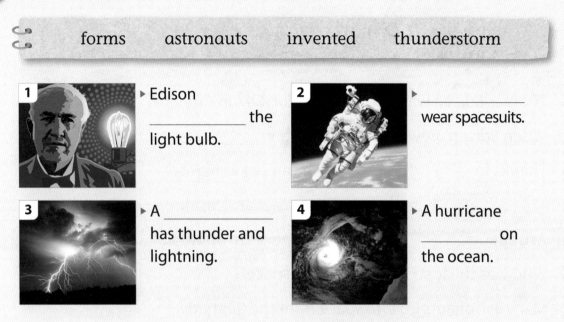

1 ▸ Edison _____ the light bulb.

2 ▸ _____ wear spacesuits.

3 ▸ A _____ has thunder and lightning.

4 ▸ A hurricane _____ on the ocean.

B Draw a circle around the right words and then write the words.

1 Thomas Edison was very _____.
                      curious   convenient

2 Space shuttles lift _____ from the Kennedy Space Center.
                 on   off

3 Storms can _____ heavy rain.
                strike   bring

4 The hurricane _____ the city.
                lifted   destroyed

C Complete the sentences with the words below.

shuttles	born	inventor	electric lights
inventions	human	explore	Space Center

1 Thomas Edison was _____ in 1847 in America.

2 When Edison grew up, he became an _____.

3 Thanks to _____, we can see at night.

4 _____ make our work easier and faster.

5 Astronauts _____ space and learn about it.

6 Who was the first _____ in space?

7 Many astronauts go into space from the Kennedy _____.

8 Space _____ lift off from the center.

D Complete the sentences with the words below.

funnel-shaped	thunder	lightning	floods
thunderstorms	forms	destroy	harmful

1 Flash! _____ strikes across the sky.

2 Boom! _____ makes a loud sound.

3 Sometimes heavy rain causes _____.

4 Storms can be _____.

5 Big _____ can make a tornado.

6 A tornado has a _____ cloud with strong winds.

7 A tornado can _____ buildings and kill people.

8 A hurricane _____ on the ocean.

34

Chapter

2

Science

Unit

05

How Do Plants Grow?

Reading Focus

- What are seeds?
- What do seeds need to grow?
- How do plants grow and change?

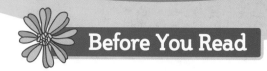
Before You Read

09

Key Words

sunflower

pea

bean

bell pepper

Seeds

strawberry

How Plants Grow

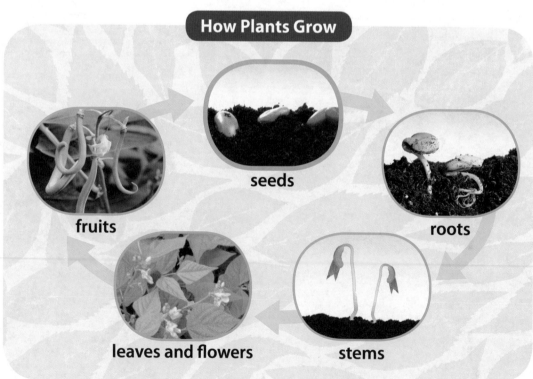

fruits

seeds

roots

leaves and flowers

stems

Power Verbs

plant
Let's **plant** seeds.

dig
He **digs** a hole.

put
He **puts** the seeds in the hole.

cover
He **covers** the hole with soil.

water
He **waters** the seeds.

become
The seeds **become** new plants.

Word Families: What Seeds Need to Grow?

What Seeds Need to Grow

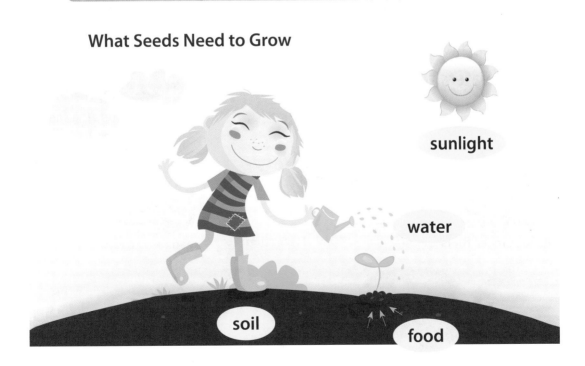

sunlight

water

soil

food

39

How Do Plants Grow?

Most plants grow from seeds.
What are the seeds in these pictures?

sunflower

peas

bell pepper

strawberry

Seeds look different, but they grow into new plants.

Johnny has some bean seeds.
He is going to plant them in his garden.

▲ Johnny plants some bean seeds in his garden.

First, he digs holes in the ground.
He puts the seeds in the holes.
Then, he covers the holes with soil.

Seeds need soil to grow.
They also need water.
So Johnny waters the seeds every day.

▲ Johnny waters the seeds every day.

the flowers make fruits

seeds

Seeds Grow into Plants

seeds with roots

leaves and flowers grow

stems grow up

Slowly, the seeds start to grow.

First, roots grow down into the soil.

Next, stems grow up.

Then, leaves and flowers begin to grow.

Last, the flowers make fruits.

These fruits have seeds.

Later, these seeds grow and become new plants.

▲ Flowers make fruits.

Check Understanding

1 Which part of a plant does each picture show?

a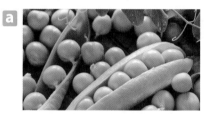

b

_____   _____

2 What does Johnny do first to plant the seeds?
a He puts the seeds in the soil.   b He digs some holes.
c He waters the seeds.

3 What do seeds need to grow?
a roots   b soil   c stems

4 A plant's flowers make _____ .
a fruits   b stems   c leaves

• **Answer the questions below.**

1 What grows into new plants? ⇨ _____ grow into new plants.

2 What grows after the stem?
   ⇨ _____ and _____ grow after the stem.

Vocabulary and Grammar Builder

A **Look, Read, and Write.**

Look at the pictures. Write the correct words.

| seeds | grow up | soil | grow down |

1  ▸ _____ grow into new plants.

2 ▸ Seeds need _____ to grow.

3  ▸ First, roots _____ into the soil.

4  ▸ Next, stems _____.

B **Grow or Grows?**

Draw a circle around the right words and then write the words.

1 Most plants _____ from seeds.

grow   grows

2 He is going to _____ seeds in his garden.

plant   plants

3 He _____ holes in the ground.

dig   digs

4 He _____ the holes with soil.

cover   covers

Unit 06

A World of Animals: Snakes

Reading Focus

- What does a snake look like?
- What are some snakes?
- How do some snakes kill other animals?

Before You Read

Key Words

A Snake's Body Parts

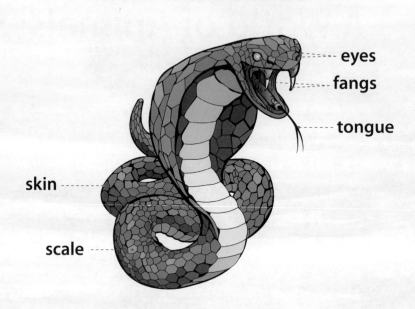

eyes

fangs

tongue

skin

scale

Snakes

anaconda

cobra

boa

rattlesnake

asp

python

Power Verbs

slither
Snakes **slither** on the ground.

lay eggs
Snakes **lay eggs**.

hatch
Snakes **hatch** from eggs.

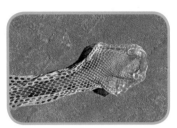

molt
Snakes **molt** once a year.

sense
Snakes **sense** with their tongues.

bite
Snakes **bite** with their fangs.

Word Families: Adjectives and Nouns

poisonous *adj.* ➡ Some snakes are poisonous.

poison *n.* ➡ Some snakes have poison.

harmful *adj.* ➡ Most snakes are not harmful.

harm *n.* ➡ Most snakes cause no harm.

45

Snakes

Look at the pictures.
What are these animals?

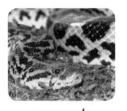

anaconda

cobra

boa

rattlesnake

They are all snakes.

Snakes are special.
They have no arms, legs, or wings.
They can't walk or run.
So how do they move?
They slither on the ground.
Snakes move their bodies back and forth.
This lets them move in all directions.

▲ Snakes slither on the ground.

Most snakes lay eggs.
More than 40 eggs hatch at one time.

Also, snakes molt at least once a year.
Then, new skin grows.

▲ Snakes molt at least once a year.
(cc by born1945)

Snakes have long tongues, too.
They use their tongues to sense other animals.
And most snakes have long fangs.
They bite with their fangs.

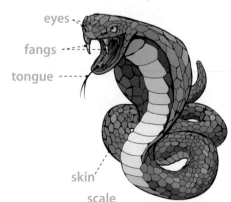

eyes

fangs

tongue

skin

scale

Some snakes are poisonous.

Poisonous snakes use poison to kill other animals.

They are very dangerous.

But most snakes are not harmful to humans.

▲ Most snakes are not harmful.

Check Understanding

1 **Which type of snake does each picture show?**

a

_____

b

_____

2 **How do snakes move?**
   a by slithering   b by running   c by walking

3 **About how often do snakes molt?**
   a once a week   b once a month   c once a year

4 **What do snakes bite with?**
   a eyes   b fangs   c tongues

• **Answer the questions below.**

1 What do snakes use to sense other animals?
   ⇨ Snakes use their _____ to sense other animals.

2 What are some snakes?
   ⇨ The _____, _____, _____, and
   _____ are all snakes.

A **Look, Read, and Write.**
Look at the pictures. Write the correct words.

> back and forth   molt   bite   slither

1  ▸ Snakes _____ on the ground.

2 ▸ Snakes can move _____.

3  ▸ Snakes _____ with their fangs.

4 ▸ Snakes _____ at least once a year.

B **Poison or Poisonous?**
Draw a circle around the right words and then write the words.

1 Some snakes are _____.
poison   poisonous

2 Some snakes use _____ to kill other animals.
poison   poisonous

3 Some snakes are _____.
danger   dangerous

4 Most snakes are not _____ to people.
harm   harmful

48

Unit 07

Amazing Changes: Butterflies

Reading Focus

- What kind of animal is a butterfly?
- How does a butterfly grow and change?

Key Words

How a Butterfly Grows

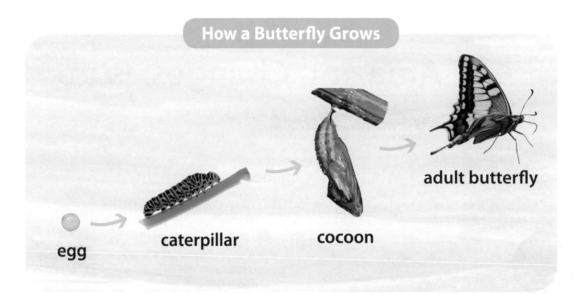

egg → caterpillar → cocoon → adult butterfly

A Butterfly's Body Parts

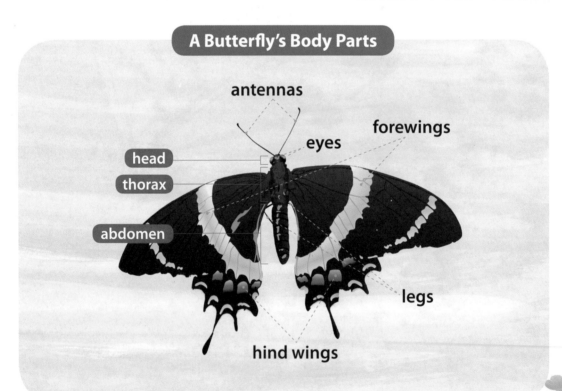

antennas

eyes

forewings

head

thorax

abdomen

legs

hind wings

Power Verbs

take a close look at
Let's take a close look at a butterfly.

fly
A butterfly flies with its wings.

grow bigger
The caterpillar grows bigger.

build
The caterpillar builds a cocoon.

come out of
A butterfly comes out of a cocoon.

Word Families: Adjectives

caterpillar — small — hungry

cocoon — hard — covering

butterfly — beautiful — adult

Butterflies

14

Every year, we can see many butterflies.
There are nearly 20,000 types of butterflies.

Let's take a close look at a butterfly.
A butterfly has three body parts.
It has a head, a thorax, and an abdomen.

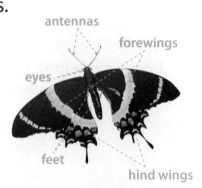

antennas

forewings

eyes

feet

hind wings

A butterfly's eyes are on its head.
It sees with its eyes.
A butterfly's antennas are also on its head.
Antennas are used for both touching and smelling.

A butterfly has six legs.
They are on its thorax.
A butterfly's wings are also on its thorax.
It flies with its wings.
A butterfly has four wings: two forewings and two hind wings.

Butterflies cannot fly from birth.
They change over time.
A butterfly begins in an egg.
Then, a caterpillar comes out of the egg.

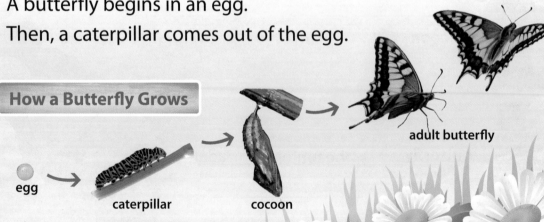

How a Butterfly Grows

egg

caterpillar

cocoon

adult butterfly

The caterpillar eats leaves and grows bigger.

Then, it builds a cocoon.

This is a hard covering.

Inside the cocoon, the caterpillar changes.

After about a week, a butterfly comes out of the cocoon.

Now, it's an adult butterfly.

▲ Cocoon is a hard covering.

▲ After about a week, a butterfly comes out of the cocoon.

Check Understanding

1   Which body part does each picture show?

a

b

_____   _____

2   What body part does a butterfly touch with?
   a its wings   b its antennas   c its eyes

3   How many wings does a butterfly have?
   a two   b four   c six

4   A _____ comes out of an egg.
   a caterpillar   b cocoon   c butterfly

• **Answer the questions below.**

1   What are the three parts of a butterfly's body?
   ⇨ They are the _____, _____, and _____.

2   What does a caterpillar do?
   ⇨ It _____ leaves and _____ bigger.

A **Look, Read, and Write.**
Look at the pictures. Write the correct words.

caterpillar   cocoon   head   comes out

1  ▸ A butterfly's antennas are on its _____.

2  ▸ A _____ is a hard covering.

3  ▸ A butterfly _____ of a cocoon.

4  ▸ A _____ changes into a butterfly.

B **At or On?**
Draw a circle around the right words and then write the words.

1 A butterfly flies _____ its wings.
with   on

2 Butterflies cannot fly _____ birth.
for   from

3 Butterflies change _____ time.
off   over

4 A caterpillar changes _____ its cocoon.
inside   outside

54

Unit 08

Birds Are Animals

Reading Focus

- What are some birds?
- What do most birds look like?
- What are some different birds?

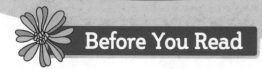

Before You Read

15

Key Words

eagle

peacock

chicken

Birds

duck

ostrich

kiwi

penguin

A Bird's Body Parts

feathers

wings

tail

beak

Power Verbs

have in common
Birds **have** feathers **in common**.

cover
Feathers **cover** a bird's body.

peck at
Birds **peck at** food with their beaks.

sit on
Birds **sit on** their eggs.

keep warm
Birds **keep** their eggs **warm**.

feed
Parent birds **feed** baby birds.

Word Families: How Birds Grow?

adult bird

eggs

How a Bird Grows

hatch

can fly

have feathers

feed

57

Birds Are Animals

16

Look at the pictures.

eagle

chicken

duck

peacock

What do they have in common?
They are all birds.
Birds are animals.
There are many different kinds of birds.

Birds have feathers.
These cover their bodies.

Birds also have wings.
Most birds use their wings to fly.

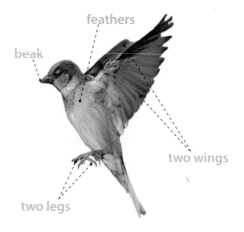
feathers
beak
two wings
two legs

Birds have beaks, too.
These are their mouths.
Birds peck at food with their beaks.

Birds lay eggs in nests.
Most birds sit on their eggs.
This keeps their eggs warm.
Later, the eggs hatch, and baby birds are born.
When birds hatch, they cannot fly.
Parent birds feed them.

▲ lay eggs in a nest

▲ hatch from eggs

Some birds are very large.
Ostriches are huge birds.
They cannot fly, but they can run very fast.
Kiwis cannot fly either.

▲ Ostriches run very fast.

▲ Kiwis cannot fly.

Check Understanding

1 **Which bird does each picture show?**

a

b

_____   _____

2 **What covers a bird's body?**
a feathers   b wings   c beaks

3 **Where do birds lay eggs?**
a On the ground   b In parks   c In nests

4 **Parent birds _____ their baby birds.**
a feed   b hatch   c peck at

• **Answer the questions below.**

1 What birds cannot fly?
⇨ _____ and _____ cannot fly.

2 How do birds eat?
⇨ Birds _____ at food with their _____.

59

Vocabulary and Grammar Builder

A **Look, Read, and Write.**
Look at the pictures. Write the correct words.

hatch	beaks	keep	feathers

1 ▸ _____ are birds' mouths.

2 ▸ Birds _____ their eggs warm.

3 ▸ Baby birds _____ from eggs.

4 ▸ Birds have _____ .

B **Cover or Hatch?**
Draw a circle around the right words and then write the words.

1 Feathers _____ a bird's body.
cover   hatch

2 Birds _____ at food with their beaks.
peck   feed

3 Birds _____ on their eggs.
fly   sit

4 Parent birds _____ baby birds.
feed   sit

Review Test 2

A Look at the pictures. Write the correct words.

slither   common   caterpillar   seeds

1  ▸ Most plants grow from _____.

2  ▸ Snakes _____ on the ground.

3  ▸ The _____ builds a cocoon.

4 ▸ Birds have feathers in _____.

B Draw a circle around the right words and then write the words.

1 First, he _____ holes in the ground.
　　　dig   digs

2 Some snakes are _____.
　　　poison   poisonous

3 A butterfly's eyes are _____ its heads.
　　　at   on

4 A caterpillar changes _____ its cocoon.
　　　inside   outside

61

C Complete the sentences with the words below.

poisonous	plant	back and forth	wings
grow up	molt	grow down	flowers

1 Johnny is going to _____ some seeds in his garden.

2 First, roots _____ into the soil.

3 Next, stems _____ .

4 Then, leaves and _____ begin to grow.

5 Snakes have no arms, legs, or _____ .

6 Snakes move their bodies _____ .

7 Snakes _____ at least once a year.

8 _____ snakes use poison to kill other animals.

D Complete the sentences with the words below.

caterpillar	feed	birth	egg
cocoon	in common	hatch	nests

1 Butterflies cannot fly from _____ .

2 A butterfly begins in an _____ .

3 Then, a _____ comes out of the egg.

4 Inside the _____ , the caterpillar changes.

5 Birds have feathers _____ .

6 Birds lay eggs in _____ .

7 Later, the eggs _____ , and baby birds are born.

8 Parent birds _____ their baby birds.

Chapter

3

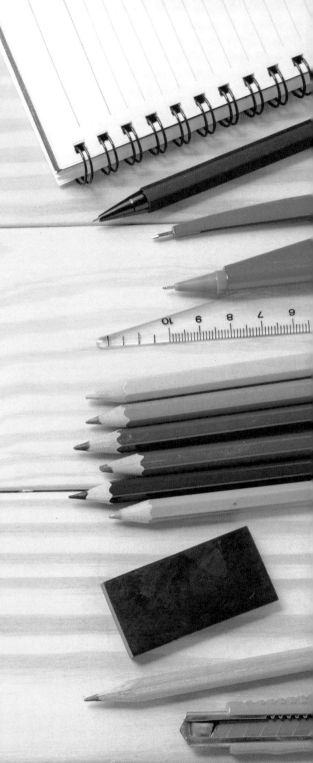

Language

★

Mathematics

★

Visual Arts

★

Music

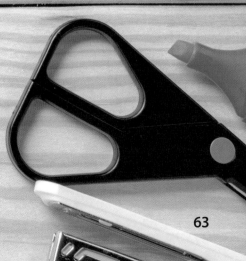

Unit 09

The City Mouse and the Country Mouse

Reading Focus

- Who is in the story?
- How are the country and city different?
- Why did the country mouse go back home?

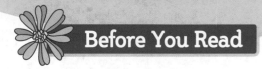

Key Words

Who Is in the Story?

the city mouse

the country mouse

cat

Meals

breakfast   lunch   dinner

dining table

Food

cheese   fruit   bread

meat   potato   cake

Power Verbs

visit
The city mouse **visited** his friend.

set the table
He **set the table**.

serve
He **served** food.

taste
He **tasted** some cheese.

return
He **returned** to his house.

arrive
They **arrived** at the house.

finish
They could not **finish** their dinner.

pass
A few minutes **passed**.

go back
He **went back** to the country.

Word Families

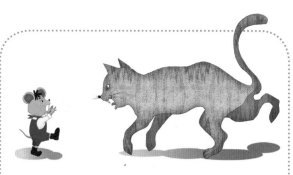

frightened = surprised

one mouse

two mice

The City Mouse and the Country Mouse

Once upon a time, there were two mice.

They were friends.

One mouse lived in a small house in the country.

The other mouse lived in a large house in the city.

One day, the city mouse went to visit his friend in the country.

The country mouse was so happy to see the city mouse.

He set the table for dinner.

He served some pieces of corn, green peas, and berries.

The city mouse looked around the table and said,

"Oh, my! This is all you have? Is this really dinner?

How can you eat such plain food every day, my friend?"

"I'm sorry," answered the country mouse.

"But this is what we eat in the

country every day," he said.

"Come with me to the city," said the city mouse.
"What is in the city?" asked the country mouse.
"There is a lot of delicious food," answered the city mouse.
"Once you have tasted all the wonderful food,
you will never want to return to the country."

So the two mice went to the city.

The mice walked for a long time.
At last, they arrived at the city mouse's home.
He lived in a very big house.
"You must be hungry. We will have dinner
soon," said the city mouse.
He invited his friend into a large kitchen.
"Help yourself. There is enough food for us," said the city mouse.

On the huge dining table, there was a lot of delicious food.
There were lots of bread and cheese.
There were lots of meat and potatoes.
There were fruits and cakes, too.

"See," said the city mouse.
"This is how we eat in the city every day."
"You were right, my friend. This is a very good dinner,"
answered the country mouse.

The two mice began to eat the dinner.
Just then, the door opened, and they
saw a cat coming.
"Run!" shouted the city mouse.
The two mice quickly ran through a
small hole in the wall.

"Whew! That was close," said the city mouse.
"Just wait here for a while, and then we can finish our dinner."

But the county mouse was very frightened.
He could not even talk.
A few minutes passed.
"Let's go back and eat," said the city mouse.
"No, thank you, my friend," said the country mouse.
"I'm going back to the country. I like my simple house.
There is not much food at my house.
But I can eat it in peace. Goodbye, my friend."
The country mouse went back to his home.

1 **Which animal does each picture show?**

a

b

_____   _____

2 **What kind of food did the country mouse serve?**
a plain food   b delicious food   c hot food

3 **What does "plain" mean?**
a delicious   b simple   c small

4 **Where did the city mouse live?**
a in a small house   b in a big house   c in a park

5 **Why did the city mouse and the country mouse run through a hole?**
a They saw a dog coming.
b They saw a cat coming.
c They saw some mice coming.

6 **Why did the country mouse decide to go back to his home?**
a He did not like the delicious food.
b There was not much food at the city mouse's house.
c He liked his simple but peaceful life in the country.

• **Answer the questions below.**

1 What did the country mouse serve to the city mouse?
⇨ He served some pieces of _____, green _____, and _____.

2 How did the country mouse feel about the cat?
⇨ He was very _____ of the cat.

Vocabulary and Grammar Builder

A **Look, Read, and Write.**
Look at the pictures. Write the correct words.

> plain   delicious   frightened   dining table

1  ▸ Dinner in the country was _____ .

2  ▸ Dinner in the city was _____ .

3 ▸ There was a big _____ .

4  ▸ The country mouse was very _____ .

B **Serveed or Served?**
Draw a circle around the past form of each verb and then write the verb.

1 The country mouse _____ food to the city mouse. (serve)
serveed   served

2 At last, they _____ at the city mouse's home. (arrive)
arrived   arriveed

3 The two mice _____ to eat the dinner. (begin)
beginned   began

4 The country mouse _____ back to his home. (go)
goed   went

Unit

Counting to 100

Reading Focus

- How high can you count?
- Can you count to 100 by tens?
- Can you count backward?

79 43 54 57 84 74 52 47
21 29 96 90 39
23 70 2 34 22 8 33 41 28 65
48 19 75 46
86 26 42 17 85 10 15 97 71
78 55 69 83 1 63 60 67 76 18
24 38 11 37 16 9 95
25 94 6 20 12 5 58 32
53 44 7 4 3 27
62 93 87 36 98 50
30 77 56 49 88 68 31
45 72 92 35 73 14
59 13 81
89 61 82 91 64 80 IOO
40 99
66 51

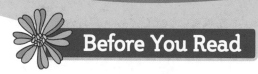

 19

Key Words

Counting by Tens

10	20	30	40	50
ten	twenty	thirty	forty	fifty
60	70	80	90	100
sixty	seventy	eighty	ninety	one hundred

Counting by Fives

5	10	15	20	25
five	ten	fifteen	twenty	twenty-five
30	35	40	45	50
thirty	thirty-five	forty	forty-five	fifty
55	60	65	70	75
fifty-five	sixty	sixty-five	seventy	seventy-five
80	85	90	95	100
eighty	eighty-five	ninety	ninety-five	one hundred

Power Verbs

continue
Let's **continue** counting.

count by tens
I can **count by tens**.

$3 \times 2 =$

find out
Let's **find out** the answer.

count by fives
I can **count by fives**.

40 39 38 37 36
35 34 33 32 31

count backward
Let's **count backward**.

20 19 18 17 16
15 14 13 12 11 10

try
Try counting backward from 20 to 10.

practice
Practice counting out loud.

50, 49, 48, 47, 46,...

be able to
He **is able to** count backward.

Word Families

1 2 3 4 5 6 7 8 9 10   **above**   What numbers are **above** 5?

1 2 3 4 5 6 7 8 9 10   **between**   Say the numbers **between** 1 and 10.

Counting to 100

You can count from 1 to 20.

One, two, three, four, five, six, seven, eight, nine, ten.

Eleven, twelve, thirteen, fourteen, fifteen.

Sixteen, seventeen, eighteen, nineteen, twenty.

What about bigger numbers?

Can you count to 100?

First, let's count from 20 to 30.

After 20, the numbers continue: 21, 22, 23, 24, 25, 26, 27, 28, 29, 30.

Twenty-one, twenty-two, twenty-three, twenty-four, twenty-five.

Twenty-six, twenty-seven, twenty-eight, twenty-nine, thirty.

Now, what numbers are above 30?

Let's count by tens and find out.

Ten, twenty, thirty, forty, fifty.

Sixty, seventy, eighty, ninety, one hundred.

10 20 30 40 50 60 70 80 90 100

Sometimes people count by fives, too.

Let's count by fives to 50.

Five, ten, fifteen, twenty, twenty-five.

Thirty, thirty-five, forty, forty-five, fifty.

5 10 15 20 25 30 35 40 45 50

Let's learn to count backward.

For example, try counting backward from 30 to 20 like this:

30, 29, 28, 27, 26, 25, 24, 23, 22, 21, 20.

Go ahead and try. You can do it.

Now, let's practice counting out loud from 1 to 100.
You should be able to say the name of
any number between 1 and 100.
Can you? Good job!

Check Understanding

1 **What does each picture show?**

a 5 10 15 20
25 30 35 40

counting _____

b 10 9 8 7
6 5 4 3

counting _____

2 **Which numbers are grouped by tens?**
a 10, 20, 30, 40, 50   **b** 5, 10, 15, 20, 25   **c** 1, 2, 3, 4, 5

3 **Which numbers are grouped by fives?**
a 10, 20, 30, 40, 50   **b** 5, 10, 15, 20, 25   **c** 1, 2, 3, 4, 5

4 **30, 29, 28, 27, 26 is counting _____.**
a by fives   **b** forward   **c** backward

• **Answer the questions below.**

1 What are the numbers from 10 to 50 counting by tens?
⇨ They are _____, _____, _____, _____,
and _____.

2 What are the numbers from 60 to 100 counting by tens?
⇨ They are _____, _____, _____, _____,
and _____ _____.

A **Look, Read, and Write.**
Look at the pictures. Write the correct words.

find out   continue   able to   fives

1

10, 11, 12, ...,
98, 99, 100

▸ Let's _____ counting from 10 to 100.

2

5 10 15 20 25
30 35 40 45 50

▸ Let's count by _____.

3
3×2 =

▸ Let's _____ the answer.

4
50, 49, 48, 47, 46,...

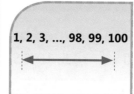

▸ Are you _____ count backward?

B **By or For?**
Draw a circle around the right words and then write the words.

10 20 30 40 50
60 70 80 90 100

1, 2, 3, ...,
98, 99, 100

1, 2, 3, ..., 98, 99, 100

10, 20, 30, 40, 50, 60,...

1 I can count _____ tens.
    by   for

2 He can count _____ 1 to 100.
    from   in

3 Say any number _____ 1 and 100.
    above   between

4 What numbers are _____ 30?
    above   between

Unit 11

What Do Artists Do?

Reading Focus

- What do artists make?
- What do artists need?
- Who are some famous artists?

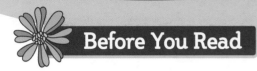

21

Key Words

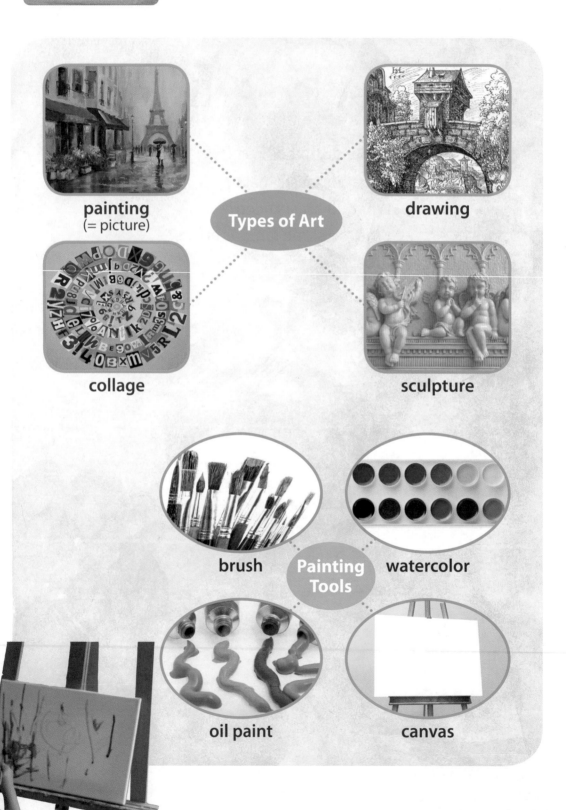

Types of Art

painting
(= picture)

drawing

collage

sculpture

Painting Tools

brush

watercolor

oil paint

canvas

Power Verbs

paint
A painter **paints** pictures.

sing
A singer can **sing** well.

draw
Some artists **draw** with pencils.

make
Some artists **make** sculptures.

Word Families: They Are All Artists

painter

singer

Artists

dancer

sculptor

What Do Artists Do?

Artists are people who make art.
Some artists paint.
Some artists sing.
Others build houses and make beautiful things.

Do you like to draw pictures?
Or do you like to build with blocks?
How about making collages?
When you do these things, you are making art.

Some artists draw with pencils on paper.
Other artists paint pictures on a canvas.

Some artists use brushes and watercolors.
Other artists use oil paints to paint pictures.
We call them painters.

▲ painting a picture

Some artists make sculptures.
We call them sculptors.

▲ making a sculpture

▲ *Mona Lisa*

Do you know any famous painters?
Let's see one of the most famous paintings
in the world.

Have you ever seen it before?
Look at her face.
Is she happy? Is she looking at you?

It is a painting by the Italian artist Leonardo da Vinci.

He painted the *Mona Lisa* around 500 years ago.

But people still enjoy looking at the picture.

▶ Leonardo da Vinci

Check Understanding

1 Which kind of art does each picture show?

a

b

_____ _____

2 What do painters use?

a blocks   b clay   c brushes

3 What is the *Mona Lisa*?

a a sculpture   b a collage   c a painting

4 A sculptor makes _____.

a sculptures   b pictures   c songs

• **Answer the questions below.**

1 Who are artists?

⇨ Artists are people who _____ _____.

2 Who painted the *Mona Lisa*?

⇨ The Italian _____ Leonardo da Vinci _____ the *Mona Lisa*.

A **Look, Read, and Write.**
Look at the pictures. Write the correct words.

> draw   painters   sing   sculptor

1  ▸ Some _____ paint pictures on a canvas.

2  ▸ Some artists _____.

3 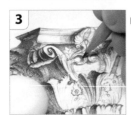 ▸ Some artists _____ with pencils on paper.

4  ▸ A _____ makes sculptures.

B **Make or Making?**
Draw a circle around the right words and then write the words.

1   When you draw a picture, you are _____ art.
make   making

2   Is she _____ at you?
look   looking

3   He is _____ a picture on a canvas.
paint   painting

4   Sculptors _____ sculptures.
make   making

Unit 12

Ballet Music

Reading Focus

- What is a ballet?
- Who is a ballerina?
- What are some famous ballets?

Key Words

Ballet

ballet dancer ballerina music dance

The Nutcracker *Swan Lake*

The Nutcracker

nutcracker

Clara prince

kingdom

Power Verbs

clap
Clap your hands.

tap
Tap your toes.

dance
They dance very well.

love to
People love to dance.

tell a story
A ballet can tell a story.

be performed
The ballet is performed every year.

come to life
A toy nutcracker comes to life.

be composed
The Nutcracker was composed
by Tchaikovsky.

Ballet Music

What do you do when you hear a fun, happy song?
Do you clap your hands?
Do you tap your toes?

▲ Dancing is moving to music.

Sometimes music can make you move.
That is dancing.
Dancing is moving to music.
Many people love to dance. Do you?

▲ Ballet is a kind of dance.

There are many kinds of dances.
Ballet is one kind.
A ballet has no singing or talking.
But it can tell a story by the movements of dancers and music.

The Nutcracker is one of the most famous ballets.
It is performed every year around Christmas.

It tells the story of a young girl's dream
on Christmas.
In a dream, a toy nutcracker comes to life
and fights a Mouse King.
Then, the nutcracker becomes a prince.
He and the girl—Clara—travel to his kingdom.
There, they watch all kinds of dancing.

The Nutcracker was composed by Tchaikovsky.
Tchaikovsky was a Russian composer.
He wrote many famous ballets.
He wrote *The Nutcracker*, *Swan Lake*, and
The Sleeping Beauty.

▲ Tchaikovsky

Check Understanding

1   **What does each picture show?**

_____   _____

2   **What is dancing?**
a moving to music   b singing to music   c listening to music

3   **What is *The Nutcracker*?**
a a famous composer   b a famous ballet   c a kingdom

4   **A ballet tells a story through the _____ of dancers.**
a songs   b movements   c voices

• **Answer the questions below.**

1 When is *The Nutcracker* performed?
⇨ It is performed _____ _____ around _____.

2 What ballets did Tchaikovsky write?
⇨ He wrote _____ _____, _____ _____, and
_____ _____ _____.

Vocabulary and Grammar Builder

A **Look, Read, and Write.**
Look at the pictures. Write the correct words.

> ballets   composer   dance   nutcracker

 **1** ▸ People love to _____.

 **2** ▸ Tchaikovsky was a Russian _____.

 **3** ▸ Tchaikovsky wrote many famous _____.

 **4** ▸ The _____ fights the Mouse King.

B **Perform or Performed?**
Draw a circle around the right words and then write the words.

1 *The Nutcracker* is _____ every year.
    perform   performed

2 They _____ *The Nutcracker* every year.
    perform   are performed

3 *The Nutcracker* was _____ by Tchaikovsky.
    compose   composed

4 Tchaikovsky _____ *The Nutcracker*.
    composed   was composed

A Look at the pictures. Write the correct words.

frightened   painted   ballet   tens

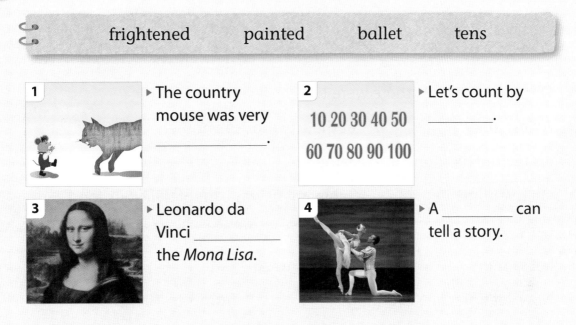

1 ▸ The country mouse was very _____.

2 10 20 30 40 50 60 70 80 90 100 ▸ Let's count by _____.

3 ▸ Leonardo da Vinci _____ the *Mona Lisa*.

4 ▸ A _____ can tell a story.

B Draw a circle around the right words and then write the words.

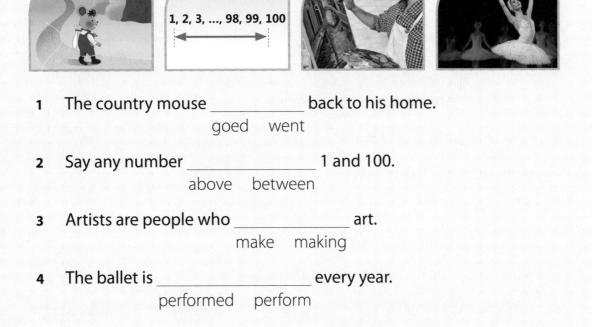

1, 2, 3, ..., 98, 99, 100

1 The country mouse _____ back to his home.
       goed   went

2 Say any number _____ 1 and 100.
      above   between

3 Artists are people who _____ art.
      make   making

4 The ballet is _____ every year.
    performed   perform

C Complete the sentences with the words below.

continue	out loud	backward	mice
dining	kitchen	able to	arrived

1 Once upon a time, there were two _____.

2 At last, they _____ at the city mouse's home.

3 He invited his friend into a large _____.

4 On the huge _____ table, there was a lot of delicious food.

5 Let's _____ counting from 20 to 30.

6 Let's count _____ from 30 to 20.

7 Now, let's practice counting _____ from 1 to 100.

8 You should be _____ say the name of any number between 1 and 100.

D Complete the sentences with the words below.

composed	comes to life	ballets	artists
watercolors	canvas	painting	dancing

1 _____ are people who make art.

2 Some artists paint pictures on a _____.

3 Some artists use brushes and _____.

4 The *Mona Lisa* is a _____ by Leonardo da Vinci.

5 _____ is moving to music.

6 *The Nutcracker* is one of the most famous _____.

7 In a dream, a toy nutcracker _____ and fights a Mouse King.

8 *The Nutcracker* was _____ by Tchaikovsky.

Word List

Word List

01 Thanks, Thomas Edison
感謝湯瑪士・愛迪生

1	**Thomas Edison**	湯瑪士・愛迪生	
2	**turn on**	打開（電燈、電風扇等）	
3	**light**	燈（光）	
4	**dark**	黑暗的	
5	**electric light**	電燈	
6	**famous**	有名的	
7	**inventor**	發明家	
8	**be born**	出生	
9	**America**	美國	
10	**curious**	好奇的	
11	**always**	總是；永遠	
12	**ask a question**	問問題	
13	**Why?**	為什麼？	
14	**Why is that?**	這是為什麼？	
15	**grow up**	成長 *過去式：grew up	
16	**become**	改變；變成 *過去式：became	

17	**call**	稱為……	
18	**invention**	發明物	
19	**invent**	發明	
20	**electric light bulb**	電燈泡	
21	**thanks to**	感謝……	
22	**at night**	在夜晚的時候	
23	**phonograph**	留聲機	
24	**listen to music**	聽音樂	
25	**stereo**	立體音響裝置	
26	**motion picture camera**	攝影機	
27	**see a movie**	看電影	
28	**more than**	比……還要多；超過……	
29	**life**	生活 *複數：lives	
30	**convenient**	便利的；方便的	
31	**more convenient**	較方便的	
32	**in the world**	世界上	
33	**work**	工作	
34	**easier**	較簡單的	

| 35 | faster | 較快的 |
| 36 | some of | 有些…… |

02 The First Man Into Space
第一位進入宇宙的人

1	space	太空;宇宙
2	like	喜歡
3	like V-ing	喜歡去做……
4	like to V	喜歡去做……
5	travel	旅行;旅遊
6	new place	陌生的地方
7	would like to	想要……
8	How about V-ing?	關於……怎麼樣?
9	travel into	到……旅行
10	astronaut	太空人
11	explore	探索
12	learn about	獲悉……
13	the first	第一
14	human	人類
15	Yuri Gagarin	尤里・加加林 (第一位進入太空的人)
16	Russian	俄國的;俄國人
17	go into	進入…… * 過去式:went into
18	for the first time	第一次
19	Kennedy Space Center	甘迺迪太空中心
20	Florida	佛羅里達州
21	USA	美國 (= United States of America)
22	space shuttle	太空梭

23	lift off	(火箭等)離地升空
24	wear	穿戴;穿著
25	spacesuit	太空衣
26	protect	保護
27	American	美國的;美國人
28	moon	月亮
29	Neil Armstrong	尼爾・阿姆斯壯
30	walk on	走在……
31	Sally Ride	莎麗・萊德
32	woman	女人;女性
33	Mae Jemison	梅・傑米森
34	African-American	非裔美國人
35	Dennis Tito	丹尼斯・蒂托
36	space tourist	太空遊客
37	travel around	環繞而行
38	Earth	地球

03 Storms
風暴

1	storm	風暴
2	look up at	抬頭看
3	sky	天空
4	cloud	雲
5	dark	黑暗的
6	come	來 * 進行式:be coming
7	flash	閃光
8	lightning	閃電
9	strike	劃過
10	across	穿過
11	boom	轟隆聲

12	thunder	雷
13	make a sound	製造出聲響
14	loud	大聲的
15	thunderstorm	大雷雨
16	sometimes	有時候
17	harmful	有害的
18	bring	帶來
19	strong wind	強風
20	heavy rain	豪雨
21	heavy snow	大雪
22	cause	造成
23	flood(s)	洪水；水災
24	stream	溪流
25	overflow	氾濫
26	be covered with	被……覆蓋
27	may	也許；可能
28	fall	降下；掉落
29	snowstorm	暴風雪
30	be called	被稱為……
31	blizzard	大風雪
32	heavily	大地；強烈地
33	so...that...	如此……以致於……
34	white	白色的

04 Tornadoes and Hurricanes
龍捲風與颶風

1	tornado	龍捲風
2	hurricane	颶風
3	begin to	開始……

4	look strange	看來異常
5	cloud	雲
6	low	低的
7	purple	紫色的
8	blow	風吹
9	hard	強烈的
10	suddenly	突然
11	loud	大聲的
12	alarm	警報
13	sound	響起
14	rush to	趕往……
15	shelter	避難所
16	be coming	即將到來
17	thunderstorm	大雷雨
18	funnel-shaped	漏斗狀的
19	spin	快速旋轉
20	like	像
21	top	陀螺
22	fast	快速地
23	can be	可以是……
24	dangerous	危險的
25	lift	抬起；舉起
26	even	甚至
27	truck	卡車
28	blow away	吹走
29	destroy	摧毀
30	building	建築物
31	kill	殺害
32	huge	巨大的
33	rainstorm	暴風雨

34	be called	被稱為……
35	form	形成
36	on the ocean	在海面上
37	move onto	移動到……之上
38	land	陸地
39	fall	下（雨、雪）
40	during	當……的時候
41	center	中心
42	the eye	颶風眼

05 How Do Plants Grow?
植物如何生長？

1	plant	植物
2	grow	生長
3	most	大部分
4	seed	種子
5	these	這些
6	picture	圖片
7	sunflower	向日葵
8	pea	豌豆
9	bell pepper	甜椒
10	strawberry	草莓
11	look different	看起來不一樣
12	grow into	長成……
13	bean	豆子
14	be going to	要（去、做等）……
15	garden	花園
16	first	第一；首先
17	dig	挖（土）

18	hole	洞
19	ground	地上
20	put	放
21	then	然後
22	cover	覆蓋
23	with soil	用泥土
24	need	需要
25	water	水；澆（水）
26	every day	每天
27	slowly	慢慢地
28	start to	開始……
29	root	根
30	grow down	向下生長
31	next	接著；下一個
32	stem	莖
33	grow up	長大
34	last	最後
35	make fruits	結果實
36	later	之後
37	become	變成；長成

06 A World of Animals: Snakes
動物世界：蛇

1	snake	蛇
2	look at	看
3	anaconda	森蚺
4	cobra	眼鏡蛇
5	boa	紅尾蚺
6	rattlesnake	響尾蛇

7	special	特別的
8	arm	手臂
9	leg	腳
10	wing	翅膀
11	walk	行走
12	run	跑
13	move	移動
14	slither	爬行
15	back and forth	來來回回地
16	let	讓
17	in all directions	所有方向
18	lay eggs	孵蛋
19	hatch	孵化
20	at one time	一次；同一時間
21	molt	脫皮
22	at least	至少
23	once a year	一年一次
24	skin	皮膚
25	tongue	舌頭
26	sense	感受
27	fang	尖牙
28	bite	咬
29	poisonous	有毒的
30	poison	毒
31	kill	殺死
32	dangerous	危險的
33	harmful	有害的
34	human	人類

07 Amazing Changes: Butterflies
蝴蝶的驚人蛻變

1	amazing	驚人的
2	butterfly	蝴蝶 ＊複數：butterflies
3	every year	每年
4	nearly	將近
5	type	種類
6	take a close look at	看仔細一點
7	body part	身體部位
8	head	頭部
9	thorax	胸部
10	abdomen	腹部
11	antenna	觸角 ＊複數：antennas
12	be used for	被用來……
13	touching	觸碰
14	smelling	嗅聞
15	wing	翅膀
16	fly	飛 ＊第三人稱單數：flies
17	forewing	（有四翼的昆蟲）前翼
18	hind wing	（有四翼的昆蟲）後翼
19	from birth	從出生起
20	change	改變；蛻變
21	over time	隨著時間的推移
22	caterpillar	毛毛蟲
23	come out of	從……出來
24	grow bigger	長大
25	build	建造
26	cocoon	蛹
27	hard	堅固的
28	covering	外衣；外層

29	inside	裡面
30	a week	一個星期；一週
31	adult	成年的

 08 **Birds Are Animals**
鳥兒也是動物

1	bird	鳥
2	eagle	鷹
3	chicken	雞
4	duck	鴨子
5	peacock	孔雀
6	have in common	共同都有……
7	different	不同的
8	kind	種類
9	feather	羽毛
10	cover	覆蓋
11	body	身體 *複數：bodies
12	beak	（鳥）喙
13	mouth	嘴巴
14	peck at	啄食
15	nest	鳥巢
16	sit on	坐在……上面
17	keep...warm	替……保溫
18	hatch	孵化
19	be born	出生
20	parent bird	親鳥
21	feed	餵食
22	ostrich	鴕鳥 *複數：ostriches
23	huge	巨大的

24	kiwi	鷸鴕
25	either	也……（用於否定句）

09 **The City Mouse and the Country Mouse**
城市老鼠和鄉下老鼠

1	city	城市
2	mouse	老鼠
3	country	鄉下
4	once upon a time	很久很久以前
5	mice	老鼠 *mouse 的複數
6	friend	朋友
7	one	其中之一的
8	live in	住在……
9	in the country	在鄉下
10	the other	另外的；其他的
11	in the city	在城市
12	one day	有一天
13	go to visit	去拜訪
14	set the table	擺放餐具
15	dinner	晚餐
16	serve	提供；招待
17	some pieces of	一些
18	corn	玉米
19	green pea	青豆
20	berry	莓 *複數 berries
21	look around	看看四周
22	plain	簡樸的
23	what	什麼

24	what we eat	我們吃的（東西）
25	come with me	跟我來
26	delicious	可口的
27	once	一次
28	taste	嚐
29	wonderful	美好的
30	return	回去
31	for a long time	很長一段時間
32	at last	最後
33	arrive at	到達……
34	must be	一定……
35	hungry	餓的
36	have dinner	吃晚餐
37	invite	邀請
38	kitchen	廚房
39	Help yourself.	請自行取用；別客氣。
40	enough	足夠的
41	dining table	餐桌
42	a lot of	很多的
43	lots of	很多的
44	bread	麵包
45	cheese	起司；乳酪
46	meat	肉
47	potato	馬鈴薯
48	fruit	水果
49	cake	蛋糕
50	just then	就在這時
51	cat	貓
52	run	跑

*過去式：ran

53	shout	大喊
54	quickly	迅速地
55	through	穿過
56	hole	洞
57	wall	牆
58	That was close.	好險。
59	wait	等待
60	for a while	一會兒
61	finish	完成
62	frightened	害怕的
63	even	甚至
64	a few minutes	幾分鐘
65	pass	經過
66	go back	回去

*過去式：went back

67	No, thank you.	不了，謝謝。
68	simple	簡單的
69	in peace	平靜的
70	goodbye	再見

10 Counting to 100
數到100

1	counting	數；計算
2	count	數；計算
3	from...to...	從……到……
4	What about...?	……怎麼樣呢？
5	bigger number	較大的數字
6	continue	繼續
7	above	在……之後
8	count by tens	數十的倍數

9	find out	找出來
10	count by fives	數5的倍數
11	count backward	倒著數
12	for example	舉例來說
13	try	試著
14	go ahead	繼續
15	go ahead and try	繼續嘗試
16	practice	練習
17	out loud	大聲
18	be able to	可以；能夠
19	any number	任何數字
20	between	在……之間
21	Good job!	好棒！；做的好！

11 What Do Artists Do?
藝術家都做些什麼？

1	artist	藝術家
2	art	藝術
3	make art	製作藝術品
4	paint	畫（畫）
5	sing	唱（歌）
6	build	建造
7	draw	畫（圖）
8	draw a picture	畫圖
9	block	積木
10	build with blocks	用積木堆疊
11	collage	拼貼畫
12	pencil	鉛筆

13	on paper	在紙上
14	paint a picture	畫圖
15	on a canvas	在畫布上
16	brush	畫筆
17	watercolor	水彩
18	oil paint	油畫
19	painter	畫家
20	sculpture	雕像
21	sculptor	雕刻家
22	famous	有名的
23	one of...	其中之一
24	the most famous	最有名的
25	painting	畫作
26	Have you ever...?	你曾經……嗎？
27	look at	看看……
28	Italian	義大利的；義大利人
29	Leonardo da Vinci	李奧那多・達文西
30	*Mona Lisa*	《蒙娜麗莎的微笑》
31	around	大約
32	still	仍然
33	enjoy V-ing	喜愛……
34	picture	畫作

12 Ballet Music
芭蕾音樂

1	ballet	芭蕾
2	fun	有趣的
3	clap	鼓掌
4	tap	輕敲

5	toe	腳趾
6	move	移動
7	dancing	舞蹈
8	love to	喜歡……
9	dance	跳舞
10	many kinds of	很多種……
11	dance	舞蹈
12	tell a story	說故事
13	movement	移動
14	dancer	舞者
15	*The Nutcracker*	《胡桃鉗》
16	perform	表演
17	be performed	被演出 * perform 的被動式
18	every year	每年
19	Christmas	聖誕節
20	young	年輕的
21	girl	女孩
22	dream	夢
23	toy	玩具
24	nutcracker	胡桃鉗
25	come to life	活過來
26	fight	戰鬥

27	Mouse King	鼠王
28	become	變成
29	prince	王子
30	Clara	克萊拉
31	travel to	漫遊
32	kingdom	王國
33	watch	看
34	compose	作（曲、詩等）
35	be composed by	是……所做 *compose的被動式
36	Tchaikovsky	柴可夫斯基
37	Russian	俄國的；俄國人
38	composer	作曲家
39	*Swan Lake*	《天鵝湖》
40	*The Sleeping Beauty*	《睡美人》

Answers and Translations

Thanks, Thomas Edison

威謝湯瑪士・愛迪生

Reading Focus 閱讀焦點

- What is an inventor? 何謂發明家？
- What does an inventor do? 發明家都做些什麼？
- How do inventors help us? 發明家對我們有什麼幫助？

Key Words 關鍵字彙

Famous Inventions 有名的發明

light bulb
燈泡

phonograph
留聲機

motion picture camera
攝影機

telephone
電話

airplane
飛機

Famous Inventors 有名的發明家

Thomas Edison
湯瑪士・愛迪生

Alexander Graham Bell
亞歷山大・格雷翰・貝爾

Orville and Wilbur Wright
(the Wright brothers)
奧維爾・萊特和韋爾伯・萊特
（萊特兄弟）

Power Verbs 核心動詞

turn on
打開（燈、音響等）

Turn on the light.
打開燈。

turn off
關閉（燈、音響等）

Turn off the light.
關掉燈。

be born
出生

He **was born** in America.
他出生在美國。

grow up
成長

He **grew up** in the country.
他在鄉下長大。

invent
發明

He **invented** the light bulb.
他發明了燈泡。

Word Families: Adjectives for Invention

相關字彙：關於「發明」的形容詞

Inventor
發明家

curious
好奇的

a **curious** boy
一個好奇的男孩

famous
有名的

a **famous** inventor
一個有名的發明家

Invention
發明

fast
快速的

a **fast** airplane
快速的飛機

convenient
方便的

a **convenient** telephone
方便的電話

Thanks, Thomas Edison 感謝湯瑪士 · 愛迪生

當四周一片黑暗，我們點亮燈光。
你知道是誰發明了電燈嗎？
就是湯瑪士 · 愛迪生。

湯瑪士 · 愛迪生是一位有名的發明家，
於 1847 年出生在美國。
他是一個充滿好奇心的男孩，
總是問很多的問題，「為什麼？」「那是為什麼？」
長大後，他成為一位發明家。

發明家創造新的事物，
我們稱這些新的事物為「發明」。

湯瑪士 · 愛迪生發明了很多東西。

他發明了電燈泡，
感謝有電燈，我們才能在黑夜中看見東西。

他發明了留聲機，
感謝有他，我們才有音響能聽見音樂。

他發明了攝影機，
感謝有他，我們現在才能有電影可以看。

湯瑪士 · 愛迪生還發明了非常多其他的東西，
他的發明超過一千種！
他的發明使我們的生活更加便利。
世界上還有很多其他的發明，
發明讓我們做事更簡單、更有效率。
你知道還有哪些發明嗎？

Check Understanding 文意測驗

1 下列圖片中分別是哪一種發明？
   a phonograph 留聲機   **b** (electric) light bulb （電）燈泡

2 湯瑪士 · 愛迪生總是問什麼問題？ **b**
   a 哪裡？   **b** 為什麼？   **c** 誰？

3 電燈對我們有什麼幫助？ **a**
   a 讓我們可以在黑夜看見東西。   **b** 讓我們有音樂可以聽。   **c** 讓我們有電影可以看。

4 湯瑪士 · 愛迪生發明了_____，我們才有音響能聽見音樂。 **b**
   a 電燈泡   **b** 留聲機   **c** 攝影機

● 回答問題

1 What does an inventor do? 發明家都做些什麼？
   ⇨ An inventor makes <u>new</u> <u>things</u>. 發明家創造新的事物。

2 How did Thomas Edison's inventions help our lives? 湯瑪士 · 愛迪生的發明對我們的生活有什麼幫助？
   ⇨ His inventions made our lives <u>more</u> <u>convenient</u>. 他的發明讓我們的生活更便利。

Vocabulary and Grammar Builder 字彙與文法練習

A 看圖填空：依照圖片選出正確的單字。

1 Please <u>turn on</u> the light. 請打開燈。

2 Edison was <u>born</u> in America. 愛迪生出生在美國。

3 Edison <u>invented</u> the light bulb. 愛迪生發明了燈泡。

4 We can listen to music with a <u>stereo</u>. 我們用音響聽音樂。

B 單字選擇：圈出正確的單字，並填入空格中。

1 Thomas Edison was very _____curious_____. 湯瑪士 · 愛迪生非常有好奇心。
   (curious) convenient

2 Inventions make our lives more _____convenient_____. 發明使我們的生活更加便利。
   curious (convenient)

3 Inventions make our work _____easier_____. 發明使我們工作更容易。
   (easier) harder

4 Airplanes help people move _____faster_____. 飛機幫助人們移動更快速。
   slower (faster)

Unit 02 The First Man Into Space

第一位進入宇宙的人

Reading Focus 閱讀焦點

- What is an astronaut? 何謂太空人？
- What do astronauts do? 太空人都做些什麼？
- Who was the first person in space? 第一位進入宇宙的人是誰？

Key Words 關鍵字彙

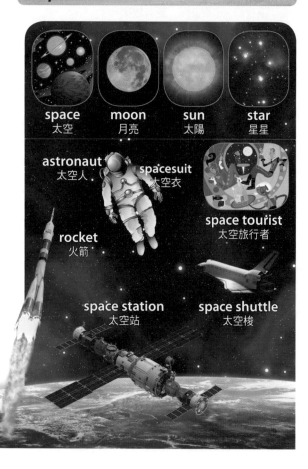

space 太空

moon 月亮

sun 太陽

star 星星

astronaut 太空人

spacesuit 太空衣

space tourist 太空旅行者

rocket 火箭

space station 太空站

space shuttle 太空梭

Power Verbs 核心動詞

travel into
到……旅行

Astronauts **travel into** space.
太空人在宇宙中旅行。

explore
探索

Astronauts **explore** the moon.
太空人探索月球。

go into
去到……

A rocket **goes into** space.
火箭飛進太空中。

lift off
（火箭等）離地升空

A space shuttle **lifts off**.
太空梭發射了。

protect
保護

Spacesuits **protect** astronauts.
太空衣保護太空人。

travel around
周遊

He **traveled around** Earth.
他繞行地球。

Word Families: The First Human in Space 相關字彙：第一位上太空的人

The First into Space
第一位進入宇宙的人

Yuri Gagarin
尤里・加加林

Neil Armstrong
尼爾・阿姆斯壯

The First Man Into Space　第一位進入宇宙的人

你喜歡到陌生的地方旅遊嗎？
你想去哪裡呢？
在太空中旅行你覺得如何？

有些人在宇宙中旅行，
他們就是太空人。
太空人探索宇宙並且獲悉相關的知識。

第一位進入宇宙的人是誰呢？
就是俄國的太空人——尤里 · 加加林。
他在 1961 年時，第一次進入太空。

這是甘迺迪太空中心，
位於美國的佛羅里達州。

許多太空人都是從這裡進入太空中，
太空梭由此發射。

太空人穿著太空衣，
在宇宙中，太空衣會保護他們。

1969 年，美國太空人第一次登上月球，
尼爾 · 阿姆斯壯是第一位在月球上行走的人。

莎麗 · 萊德是第一位進入宇宙的美國女性；
而梅 · 傑米森是第一位進入太空的非裔美國女性。
丹尼斯 · 蒂托是第一位太空旅行者，
他在 2001 年時繞行了地球。

Check Understanding　文意測驗

1　下列圖片中分別是什麼？
　　a astronaut 太空人　　　b space shuttle 太空梭

2　太空人去哪裡探索？　b
　　a 太空中心　　　　b 宇宙　　　　c 太空衣

3　太空人穿什麼？　a
　　a 太空衣　　　　b 太空中心　　　　c 太空梭

4　第一位在月球上行走的人是_____。　a
　　a 尼爾 · 阿姆斯壯　　b 尤里 · 加加林　　c 莎麗 · 萊德

● 回答問題

1　Who was the first human in space?　第一位進入太空的人是誰？
　　⇨ Yuri Gagarin was the first human in space.　尤里 · 加加林是第一位進入太空的人。

2　Where is the Kennedy Space Center?　甘迺迪太空中心在哪裡？
　　⇨ It is in Florida in the USA.　它位於美國佛羅里達州。

Vocabulary and Grammar Builder　字彙與文法練習

Ⓐ 看圖填空：依照圖片選出正確的單字。

1　Astronauts wear spacesuits.　太空人穿著太空衣。

2　Spacesuits protect astronauts in space.　太空衣可以在宇宙中保護太空人。

3　Neil Armstrong explored the moon in 1969.　尼爾 · 阿姆斯壯在 1969 年時探索了月球。

4　A space shuttle lifts off.　太空梭發射。

Ⓑ 介系詞：圈出正確的單字，並填入空格中。

1　Astronauts travel ___into___ space.　太空人到宇宙中旅行。
　　　　　　　on　(into)

2　Space shuttles lift ___off___ from the Kennedy Space Center.　太空梭從甘迺迪太空中心發射。
　　　　　　　on　(off)

3　American astronauts went to the moon ___for___ the first time in1969.　美國太空人在 1969 年第一次登上月球。
　　　　　　　(for)　to

4　The first space tourist traveled ___around___ Earth in 2001.　第一位太空旅行者於 2001 年繞行地球。
　　　　　　　off　(around)

Storms

風暴

Reading Focus 閱讀焦點

• What is a storm? 何謂風暴？

• What is a blizzard? 大風雪是怎麼樣的？

• How can storms hurt people? 風暴如何傷害人們？

Key Words 關鍵字彙

Storms
風暴

thunderstorm
大雷雨

rainstorm
暴風雨

snowstorm
暴風雪

lightning
閃電

flood
洪水；水災

blizzard
大風雪

thunder
打雷

strong wind
強風

Power Verbs 核心動詞

strike
打；擊

Lightning can **strike** trees.
閃電會擊中樹木。

make a sound
製造聲響

Thunder **makes a** loud sound.
打雷會有很大的聲音。

bring
帶來

Storms can **bring** heavy rain.
風暴會夾帶豪雨。

cause
造成

Storms can **cause** floods.
風暴會造成洪水。

overflow
氾濫

Some rivers **overflow**.
有些河川氾濫成災。

fall
降下；掉落

Snow **falls** in the winter.
雪花在冬天降下。

Word Families: The Adjectives for Storms 相關字彙：風暴的形容詞

dark
黑暗

loud
大聲的

strong
強烈的

heavy
大的；強烈的

dark clouds
烏雲

loud sounds
很大的聲音

strong winds
強風

heavy rain
豪雨

harmful
有害的

Storms can be **harmful**.
風暴是有傷害性的。

Storms　風暴

抬頭看看天空，
那又大又黑的雲，
暴風就要來了。

稍縱即逝的閃光，閃電劃破天空。
轟隆！雷發出巨大的隆隆聲。
這就是大雷雨。

有時候風暴會侵襲我們，
風暴會造成傷害，
風暴會挾帶強風，
風暴也會帶來大雨或大雪。

大雷雨會挾帶打雷、閃電、豪雨。
有時候閃電會擊中樹木或是高聳的建築物，
有時候豪雨會造成洪水，
河川及溪流氾濫成災，
陸地被水淹沒。

當天氣冷冽，可能會降下大雪，
強大的暴風雪也被稱為大風雪，
大風雪伴隨來狂風，
在大風雪中，
強烈的風雪會使人們只看得到白茫茫的一片。

Check Understanding　文意測驗

1　下列圖片中分別是哪一種風暴？
　　a thunderstorm 大雷雨　　**b** snowstorm / blizzard 暴風雪 / 大風雪

2　打雷會怎麼樣？　**a**
　　a 製造很大的聲響。　　**b** 擊中樹木。　　**c** 造成洪水。

3　豪雨會造成什麼災情？　**b**
　　a 強風　　**b** 洪水　　**c** 大風雪

4　強大的暴風雪叫作_____。　**c**
　　a 大雷雨　　**b** 暴風雨　　**c** 大風雪

● 回答問題

1　What does a thunderstorm have?　大雷雨會帶來什麼？
　　⇨ A thunderstorm has thunder, lightning, and heavy rain.　大雷雨會帶來打雷、閃電、豪雨。

2　What does a blizzard have?　大風雪會帶來什麼？
　　⇨ A blizzard has strong winds and heavy snow.　大風雪會挾帶強風和大雪。

Vocabulary and Grammar Builder　字彙與文法練習

Ⓐ 看圖填空：依照圖片選出正確的單字。

1　A thunderstorm has thunder and lightning.　大雷雨挾帶打雷與閃電。

2　Rivers and streams overflow.　河川及溪流氾濫成災。

3　Lightning can strike trees and buildings.　閃電會擊中樹木及建築物。

4　A blizzard is a big snowstorm.　大風雪就是強大的暴風雪。

Ⓑ 單字選擇：圈出正確的單字，並填入空格中。

1　Thunder makes a ___loud___ sound.　打雷製造很大的聲響。
　　(loud) dark

2　___Heavy___ rain can cause a flood.　豪雨會造成洪水。
　　Strong (Heavy)

3　A blizzard has ___strong___ winds.　大風雪帶來強風。
　　(strong) heavy

4　Storms can be ___harmful___.　風暴會造成傷害。
　　(harmful) dark

Unit 04

Tornadoes and Hurricanes

龍捲風與颶風

Reading Focus 閱讀焦點

- What is a tornado? 什麼是龍捲風？
- What is a hurricane? 什麼是颶風？
- How are these storms dangerous? 這些風暴是如何的危險？

Key Words 關鍵字彙

Tornado
龍捲風

funnel-shaped cloud
漏斗狀的雲

twister
旋風

tornado warning
龍捲風警告

tornado alarm
龍捲風警報

tornado shelter
龍捲風避難所

Hurricane
颶風

the eye
颶風眼

Power Verbs 核心動詞

rush
狂奔；急衝

People **rush** to shelter.
人們湧進避難所。

spin
旋轉

A tornado **spins** like a top.
龍捲風像陀螺一樣旋轉。

top
陀螺

lift
舉起；抬起

A tornado can **lift**
many things.
龍捲風可以捲起很多東西。

blow away
吹走

A tornado can
blow away a house.
龍捲風可以把房子吹走。

destroy
摧毀

The hurricane
destroyed the city.
颶風摧毀城市。

form
形成

A hurricane **forms**
on the ocean.
颶風在海面上形成。

Word Families: The Adjectives for Tornados 相關字彙：龍捲風的形容詞

strange
奇怪的
➡ **The sky looks strange.**
天空看起來很奇怪。

dangerous
危險的
➡ **A hurricane can be dangerous.**
颶風是危險的。

funnel-shaped
漏斗狀的
➡ **A tornado has a funnel-shaped cloud.**
龍捲風有漏斗狀的雲。

Tornadoes and Hurricanes 龍捲風與颶風

天空看起來開始異常了，
雲很低又泛著紫紅色，
風也開始變強了。
突然，警鈴大聲響起，
人們湧進避難所中，
龍捲風就要來了。

巨大的雷雨會變成龍捲風，
龍捲風是漏斗狀的雲，挾帶著強風，
那些雲就像陀螺一樣旋轉。

龍捲風的風速很快，
是非常危險的。

龍捲風可以捲起很多東西，
甚至可以捲起卡車並且將它們吹走。
龍捲風會摧毀建築物，奪走人命。

巨大的暴風雨稱為颶風，
它帶來強勁的風勢。
颶風在海面上形成，
但是它常常移動到陸地上，
挾帶著豪雨。
颶風的中心點稱為颶風眼。

Check Understanding 文意測驗

1 下列圖片中分別是什麼風暴？
a tornado 龍捲風　b hurricane 颶風

2 龍捲風的雲看起來像什麼？ b
a 圓　　　b 漏斗　　　c 眼睛

3 巨大的暴風雨稱為_____。 b
a 龍捲風　　b 颶風　　c 海洋

4 颶風的_____稱為颶風眼。 a
a 中心　　b 旁邊　　c 頂端

● 回答問題

1 Where do people go during a tornado? 龍捲風來的時候，人們會去哪裡？
⇨ People go to shelter. 人們逃至避難所。

2 What does a hurricane have? 颶風會帶來什麼？
⇨ A hurricane has very strong winds and heavy rain. 颶風會帶來強風和豪雨。

Vocabulary and Grammar Builder 字彙與文法練習

A 看圖填空：依照圖片選出正確的單字。
1 A tornado spins like a top. 龍捲風像陀螺一樣旋轉。
2 People rush to shelter. 人們湧進避難所。
3 A tornado can blow away a house. 龍捲風可以把房子吹走。
4 The center of a hurricane is called the eye. 颶風的中心點稱為颶風眼。

B 單字選擇：圈出正確的單字，並填入空格中。
1 The sky begins to look ___strange___. 天空開始看起來異常。
strange dangerous
2 A hurricane can be very ___dangerous___. 颶風是很危險的。
safe dangerous
3 A tornado has a ___funnel-shaped___ cloud. 龍捲風有漏斗狀的雲。
funnel-shaped loud
4 When a tornado is coming, the wind begins to blow ___hard___.
soft hard
當龍捲風來的時候，風會開始變強。

111

Unit 05

How Do Plants Grow?

植物如何生長？

Reading Focus 閱讀焦點

- What are seeds? 什麼是種子？
- What do seeds need to grow? 種子的成長需要什麼？
- How do plants grow and change? 植物如何成長和改變？

Key Words 關鍵字彙

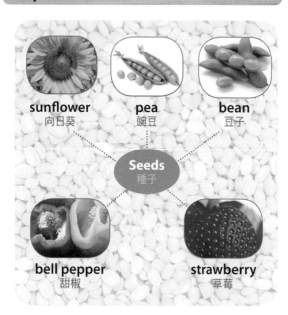

sunflower 向日葵

pea 豌豆

bean 豆子

Seeds 種子

bell pepper 甜椒

strawberry 草莓

How Plants Grow
植物如何生長

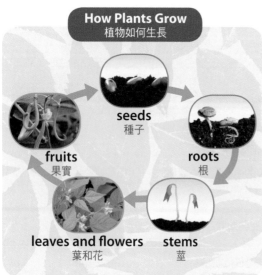

fruits 果實

seeds 種子

roots 根

leaves and flowers 葉和花

stems 莖

Power Verbs 核心動詞

plant 種植
Let's **plant** seeds.
讓我們種下這些種子。

dig 挖（土）
He **digs** a hole.
他挖了一個洞。

put 放
He **puts** the seeds in the hole.
他將種子放進洞裡。

cover 覆蓋
He **covers** the hole with soil.
他在洞上覆蓋泥土。

water 澆（水）
He **waters** the seeds.
他幫種子澆水。

become 改變
The seeds **become** new plants.
種子變成一株新的植物。

Word Families: What Seeds Need to Grow
相關字彙：植物的成長需要什麼

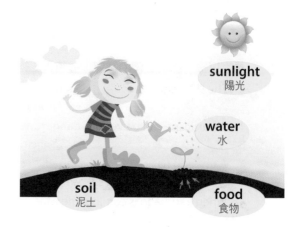

sunlight 陽光

water 水

soil 泥土

food 食物

How Do Plants Grow? 植物如何生長？

大部分的植物都是從種子開始成長，
這些圖片中有哪些種子？

向日葵　豌豆　甜椒　草莓

種子看起來不同，可是它們都會長成一株新的植物。

強尼有一些豆子的種子，
他要把它們種在花園裡，

首先，他在地上挖了一些洞，
他把種子放進洞裡。
然後他在洞上覆蓋泥土。

種子需要土壤才能生長，
而且它們也需要水，
所以強尼每天都幫這些種子澆水。

漸漸地，種子開始成長，
一開始，根向下紮進泥土裡，
接著，莖長出來了，
然後，葉子和花開始生長。

最後，花結出了果實，
這些果實含有種子，
之後，這些種子又會長成新的植物。

Check Understanding 文意測驗

1　下列圖片中分別是植物的什麼部分？
　　a seed(s) 種子　　　b fruit(s) 果實

2　強尼在播種的時候做的第一件事是什麼？ b
　　a 他把種子放進土裡。　　b 他挖了一些洞。　　c 他幫種子澆水。

3　種子需要什麼才能生長？ b
　　a 根　　　　　　b 土壤　　　　　　c 莖

4　植物的花會結_____。 a
　　a 果實　　　　　b 莖　　　　　　c 葉子

● 回答問題

1　What grows into new plants? 什麼會長成新的植物？
　　⇨ Seeds grow into new plants. 種子長成新的植物。

2　What grows after the stem? 什麼在莖之後開始生長？
　　⇨ Leaves and flowers grow after the stem. 葉子和花在莖之後開始生長。

Vocabulary and Grammar Builder 字彙與文法練習

🅐 看圖填空：依照圖片選出正確的單字。

1　Seeds grow into new plants. 種子長成新的植物。

2　Seeds need soil to grow. 種子生長需要土壤。

3　First, roots grow down into the soil. 一開始，根向下紮進泥土裡。

4　Next, stems grow up. 接著，莖長出來了。

🅑 第三人稱單數：圈出正確的單字，並填入空格中。

1　Most plants ____grow____ from seeds. 大部分的植物都是從種子開始成長。
　　　　(grow) grows

2　He is going to ____plant____ seeds in his garden. 他要把種子種在花園裡。
　　　　　　(plant) plants

3　He __digs__ holes in the ground. 他在地上挖了一些洞。
　　　dig (digs)

4　He ____covers____ the holes with soil. 他在洞上覆蓋泥土。
　　　cover (covers)

Unit 06

A World of Animals: Snakes

動物世界：蛇

Reading Focus 焦點閱讀

- What does a snake look like? 蛇看起來是什麼樣子？
- What are some snakes? 蛇有哪些？
- How do some snakes kill other animals? 蛇如何獵殺其他動物？

Key Words 關鍵字彙

A Snake's Body Parts
蛇的身體部位

eyes 眼睛
fangs 尖牙
tongue 舌頭
skin 皮膚
scale 鱗片

Snakes 蛇

anaconda 森蚺
cobra 眼鏡蛇
boa 紅尾蚺

rattlesnake 響尾蛇
asp 角蝰
python 蟒蛇

Power Verbs 核心動詞

slither
連走帶跑地滑；滑溜

Snakes **slither** on the ground.
蛇在地上爬行。

lay eggs
孵蛋

Snakes **lay eggs**.
蛇會孵蛋。

hatch
孵化

Snakes **hatch** from eggs.
蛇從蛋裡孵化出來。

molt
脫皮

Snakes **molt** once a year.
蛇一年脫一次皮。

sense
感覺

Snakes **sense** with their tongues.
蛇靠舌頭感覺事物。

bite
咬

Snakes **bite** with their fangs.
蛇用牠們的尖牙咬東西。

Word Families: Adjectives and Nouns 相關字彙：形容詞及名詞

poisonous 有毒的	*adj.* ⇒	Some snakes are poisonous. 有些蛇是有毒的。
poison 毒	*n.* ⇒	Some snakes have poison. 有些蛇有毒。
harmful 有害的	*adj.* ⇒	Most snakes are not harmful. 大部分的蛇都是無害的。
harm 傷害	*n.* ⇒	Most snakes cause no harm. 大部分的蛇不會造成傷害。

Snakes 蛇

看看這些圖片，
牠們是什麼動物？

森蚺　眼鏡蛇　紅尾蚺　響尾蛇

牠們都是蛇。

蛇是很特別的動物，
牠們沒有手、沒有腳，也沒有翅膀，
牠們不能走、不能跑，
那牠們到底是如何移動的呢？
牠們在地上爬行，
蛇來來回回扭動牠們的身體，
就能讓牠們隨心所欲往任何方向移動。

大部分的蛇都會孵蛋，
一次可以孵化超過 40 顆蛋。

蛇一年至少會脫一次皮，
然後長出新的皮膚。

蛇還有很長的舌頭，
牠們靠舌頭感覺其他動物。
大部分的蛇都有長長的尖牙，
牠們用尖牙去咬東西。

有些蛇有毒，
毒蛇利用毒液去獵殺其他動物，
牠們非常危險。
不過，其實大部分的蛇對人類都是無害的。

Check Understanding 文意測驗

1 下列圖片中分別是哪一種蛇？
   a <u>rattlesnake</u> 響尾蛇　　**b** <u>cobra</u> 眼鏡蛇

2 蛇如何移動？　**a**
   a 滑溜地爬行　　**b** 跑　　**c** 走

3 蛇大概多久脫一次皮？　**c**
   a 一個禮拜一次　　**b** 一個月一次　　**c** 一年一次

4 蛇用什麼咬東西？　**b**
   a 眼睛　　**b** 毒牙　　**c** 舌頭

● 回答問題

1 What do snakes use to sense other animals?　蛇用什麼感覺其他動物？
   ⇨ Snakes use their <u>tongues</u> to sense other animals.　蛇用牠們的舌頭感覺其他動物。

2 What are some snakes?　蛇有哪些種類？
   ⇨ The <u>anaconda</u>, <u>cobra</u>, <u>boa</u>, and <u>rattlesnake</u> are all snakes.
   森蚺、眼鏡蛇、紅尾蚺、響尾蛇都是蛇。

Vocabulary and Grammar Builder 字彙與文法練習

A 看圖填空：依照圖片選出正確的單字。

1 Snakes <u>slither</u> on the ground.　蛇在地上爬行。

2 Snakes can move <u>back and forth</u>.　蛇來來回回地扭動。

3 Snakes <u>bite</u> with their fangs.　蛇牠們的用尖牙咬東西。

4 Snakes <u>molt</u> at least once a year.　蛇至少一年脫一次皮。

B 名詞與形容詞：圈出正確的單字，並填入空格中。

1 Some snakes are ___poisonous___.　有些蛇是有毒的。
   poison　(poisonous)

2 Some snakes use ___poison___ to kill other animals.　有些蛇用毒液獵殺其他動物。
   (poison)　poisonous

3 Some snakes are ___dangerous___.　有些蛇是很危險的。
   danger　(dangerous)

4 Most snakes are not ___harmful___ to people.　大部分的蛇對人是無害的。
   harm　(harmful)

Unit 07

Amazing Changes: Butterflies

蝴蝶的驚人蛻變

Reading Focus 閱讀焦點

- What kind of animal is a butterfly? 蝴蝶是什麼樣的動物？
- How does a butterfly grow and change? 蝴蝶如何成長及蛻變？

Key Words 關鍵字彙

How a Butterfly Grows
蝴蝶的成長

egg
卵

caterpillar
毛毛蟲

cocoon
蛹

adult butterfly
成蝶

A Butterfly's Body Parts
蝴蝶的身體構造

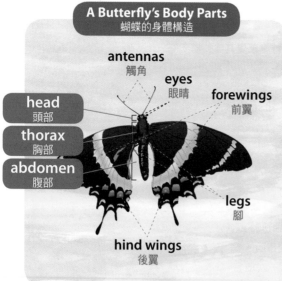

antennas
觸角

eyes
眼睛

forewings
前翼

head
頭部

thorax
胸部

abdomen
腹部

legs
腳

hind wings
後翼

Power Verbs 核心動詞

take a close look at
仔細看

Let's **take a close look at** a butterfly.
讓我們仔細來看一看蝴蝶。

fly
飛

A butterfly **flies** with its wings.
蝴蝶靠翅膀飛行。

grow bigger
長大

The caterpillar **grows bigger**.
毛毛蟲長大了。

build
建造

The caterpillar **builds** a cocoon.
毛毛蟲建造了一個蛹。

come out of
從⋯⋯出來

A butterfly **comes out of** a cocoon.
蝴蝶破蛹而出。

Word Families: Adjectives
相關字彙：形容詞

caterpillar 毛毛蟲	small 小的	hungry 餓的
cocoon 蛹	hard 堅固的	covering 覆蓋的
butterfly 蝴蝶	beautiful 美麗的	adult 成年的

Butterflies 蝴蝶

每年我們都可以看到很多蝴蝶，
世界上的蝴蝶種類將近兩萬種。

讓我們來仔細地看一看蝴蝶，
蝴蝶的身體分成三個部分，
分別是頭部、胸部和腹部。

蝴蝶的頭部有眼睛，
牠用眼睛觀看事物。
蝴蝶的頭部還長有觸角，
用來觸碰及嗅聞事物。

蝴蝶有六隻腳，
長在胸部下方；
而蝴蝶的翅膀長在胸部的上方，

蝴蝶靠翅膀飛行。
蝴蝶有四隻翅膀：兩隻前翼、兩隻後翼。

蝴蝶並不是一出生就會飛，
而是隨著時間蛻變。
蝴蝶一開始只是一顆卵，
然後，卵孵出了毛毛蟲。

毛毛蟲吃葉子，然後越長越大，
接著建造了一個蛹，
那是一層堅固的外衣。
在蛹中，毛毛蟲蛻變了。
一個禮拜之後，蝴蝶破蛹而出，
現在牠是一隻美麗的成蝶了。

Check Understanding 文意測驗

1 下列圖片中分別是蝴蝶的哪一個部位？
   a wings 翅膀   b antennas 觸角

2 蝴蝶用哪個部位觸碰？ b
   a 翅膀   b 觸角   c 眼睛

3 蝴蝶有幾隻翅膀？ b
   a 兩隻   b 四隻   c 六隻

4 卵孵出了_____。 a
   a 毛毛蟲   b 蛹   c 蝴蝶

● 回答問題

1 What are the three parts of a butterfly's body? 蝴蝶的身體分為哪三部分？
   ⇨ They are the head, thorax, and abdomen. 分為頭部、胸部和腹部。

2 What does a caterpillar do? 毛毛蟲都做些什麼？
   ⇨ It eats leaves and grows bigger. 毛毛蟲吃葉子，然後越長越大。

Vocabulary and Grammar Builder 字彙與文法練習

Ⓐ 看圖填空：依照圖片選出正確的單字。

1 A butterfly's antennas are on its head. 蝴蝶的觸角在頭上。

2 A cocoon is a hard covering. 蛹是一層堅固的外衣。

3 A butterfly comes out of a cocoon. 蝴蝶破蛹而出。

4 A caterpillar changes into a butterfly. 毛毛蟲蛻變成蝴蝶。

Ⓑ 介系詞：圈出正確的單字，並填入空格中。

1 A butterfly flies __with__ its wings. 蝴蝶靠翅膀飛行。
   (with) on

2 Butterflies cannot fly __from__ birth. 蝴蝶不是一出生就會飛。
   for (from)

3 Butterflies change __over__ time. 蝴蝶會隨著時間蛻變。
   off (over)

4 A caterpillar changes __inside__ its cocoon. 毛毛蟲在蛹中蛻變。
   (inside) outside

Unit 08 Birds Are Animals

鳥兒也是動物

Reading Focus 閱讀焦點

- What are some birds? 鳥有哪些？
- What do most birds look like? 大部分的鳥兒看起來是什麼樣子？
- What are some different birds? 有哪些不同的鳥兒？

Key Words 關鍵字彙

eagle
鷹

peacock
孔雀

Birds
鳥兒

chicken
雞

duck
鴨子

ostrich
鴕鳥

kiwi
鷸鴕

penguin
企鵝

A Bird's Body Parts
鳥的身體構造

feathers
羽毛

wings
翅膀

beak
鳥喙

tail
尾巴

Power Verbs 核心動詞

have in common
有……（共通點）

Birds **have** feathers
in common.
鳥兒都有羽毛。

peck at
（用嘴）啄食

Birds **peck at** food with
their beaks.
鳥兒用喙啄食食物。

keep warm
替……保溫

Birds **keep** their eggs
warm.
鳥兒會替牠們的蛋保溫。

cover
覆蓋

Feathers **cover**
a bird's body.
鳥兒的身體覆蓋著羽毛。

sit on
坐在……上面

Birds **sit on** their eggs.
鳥兒坐在牠們的蛋上。

feed
餵食；餵養

Parent birds **feed** baby
birds.
親鳥餵養幼鳥。

Word Families: How Birds Grow
相關字彙：鳥兒如何成長

adult bird
成鳥

eggs
蛋

hatch
孵化

How a Bird Grows
鳥兒的成長

can fly
會飛了

have feathers
長出羽毛

feed
餵養

Birds Are Animals 鳥兒也是動物

看看這些圖片，

鷹　　雞　　鴨子　　孔雀

牠們的共同特徵是什麼？
牠們都是鳥類，
鳥類也是動物，
世界上有很多種不同的鳥兒。

鳥兒有羽毛，
羽毛覆蓋牠們的身體。

鳥兒也有翅膀，
大部分的鳥兒都可以用牠們的翅膀飛翔。

鳥兒也有喙，
喙就是鳥兒的嘴巴，
牠們用喙啄食食物。

鳥兒會在巢裡頭孵蛋，
大部分的鳥兒會坐在蛋上，
讓蛋保持溫暖。
之後，蛋會孵化，幼鳥就出生了。
當幼鳥剛出生時，牠們還不會飛，
親鳥會餵養牠們。

有些鳥的體型很大，
鴕鳥就是巨大的鳥類，
牠們無法飛行，但是牠們跑得很快。
鷸鴕也是不會飛的鳥類。

Chapter 2

Unit 08

Birds Are Animals

Check Understanding 文意測驗

1　下列圖片中分別是什麼鳥？
　　a **eagle** 鷹　　　　　　**b** **peacock** 孔雀

2　鳥兒的身體覆蓋著什麼？　**a**
　　a 羽毛　　　　　　**b** 翅膀　　　　　　**c** 喙

3　鳥兒在哪裡孵蛋？　**c**
　　a 在地上　　　　　**b** 在公園。　　　　**c** 在巢裡。

4　親鳥會＿＿＿＿牠們的幼鳥。　**a**
　　a 餵養　　　　　　**b** 孵化　　　　　　**c** 啄食

● 回答問題

1　What birds cannot fly?　什麼鳥不會飛？
　　⇨ **Ostriches** and **kiwis** cannot fly. 鴕鳥和鷸鴕不會飛。（chicken 雞, duck 鴨子）

2　How do birds eat?　鳥兒如何吃東西？
　　⇨ Birds **peck** at food with their **beaks**. 鳥兒用喙啄食食物。

Vocabulary and Grammar Builder 字彙與文法練習

A 看圖填空：依照圖片選出正確的單字。

1　**Beaks** are birds' mouths. 喙就是鳥兒的嘴巴。

2　Birds **keep** their eggs warm. 鳥兒幫蛋保溫。

3　Baby birds **hatch** from eggs. 蛋孵化出幼鳥。

4　Birds have **feathers**. 鳥兒有羽毛。

B 單字選擇：圈出正確的單字，並填入空格中。

1　Feathers ＿＿**cover**＿＿ a bird's body. 鳥兒的身體覆蓋著羽毛。
　　（cover） hatch

2　Birds ＿＿**peck**＿＿ at food with their beaks. 鳥兒用喙啄食食物。
　　（peck） feed

3　Birds ＿＿**sit**＿＿ on their eggs. 鳥兒坐在牠們的蛋上。
　　fly （sit）

4　Parent birds ＿＿**feed**＿＿ baby birds. 親鳥餵養幼鳥。
　　（feed） sit

119

Unit 09 The City Mouse and the Country Mouse

城市老鼠和鄉下老鼠

Reading Focus 閱讀焦點

- Who is in the story? 故事裡有什麼角色？
- How are the country and city different? 鄉下和城市有什麼不一樣？
- Why did the country mouse go back home? 為什麼鄉下老鼠要回家去？

Key Words 關鍵字彙

Who Is in the Story?
故事裡有什麼角色？

the city mouse 城市老鼠

the country mouse 鄉下老鼠

cat 貓

Meals
膳食

breakfast 早餐　　lunch 午餐　　dinner 晚餐

dining table 餐桌

Food
食物

cheese 起司　　fruit 水果　　bread 麵包

meat 肉　　potato 馬鈴薯　　cake 蛋糕

Power Verbs 核心動詞

visit
拜訪

The city mouse **visited** his friend.
城市老鼠去拜訪他的朋友。

set the table
擺放（佈置）餐具（桌）

He **set the table**.
他把餐桌佈置好。

serve
提供；招待

He **served** food.
他招待食物。

taste
嚐

He **tasted** some cheese.
他嚐了一點起司。

return
回（去、來、到）

He **returned** to his house.
他回到他家。

arrive
到達

They **arrived** at the house.
他們到了那棟房子。

finish
完成

They could not **finish** their dinner.
他們無法吃完他們的晚餐。

pass
經過

A few minutes **passed**.
幾分鐘過去了。

go back
回（去、來、到）

He **went back** to the country.
他回到鄉下。

Word Families 相關字彙

frightened = surprised
受驚的；驚訝的

one mouse
一隻老鼠

two mice
兩隻老鼠

The City Mouse and the Country Mouse 城市老鼠和鄉下老鼠

很久很久以前，有兩隻老鼠，
他們是好朋友。
其中一隻住在鄉下的小房子裡，
另外一隻住在城市的大房子裡。

有一天，城市老鼠去鄉下拜訪他的朋友，
鄉下老鼠看到城市老鼠非常開心。
他佈置好餐桌，準備晚餐，
他準備了一些玉米、豌豆和莓子來招待城市老鼠。

城市老鼠掃視了餐桌後，說道：
「喔，我的天！你就吃這些東西？你的晚餐就這樣？我的朋友，你怎麼能夠每天都吃這麼寒酸的東西？」
「我很抱歉。」鄉下老鼠回答：
「但我們鄉下每天就是吃這些東西。」

「跟我到城市裡去吧。」城市老鼠說。
「城市裡有什麼？」鄉下老鼠問。
「那裡有好多好吃的東西。」城市老鼠回答道：
「只要你嚐過一次那些美食，
你就永遠不會想要回鄉下了。」

兩隻老鼠於是往城市出發。

他們走了好久，
最後，他們到了城市老鼠的家，
他住在一間非常大的房子裡。
「你一定餓了吧，我們馬上就可以吃晚餐了。」
城市老鼠說。
他邀請他的朋友進到一間很大的廚房。
「別客氣，這裡有足夠的食物讓我們吃個飽。」
城市老鼠說。
在偌大的餐桌上，擺滿了好多可口的食物。

有很多麵包和起司，
有很多肉和馬鈴薯，
還有好多水果和蛋糕。

「看！」城市老鼠說，
「這些就是我每天在城市裡吃的食物。」
「你是對的，我的朋友，你的晚餐真是豐盛。」
鄉下老鼠回答。

兩隻老鼠剛開始吃晚餐，
就在此時，門打開了，他們看見一隻貓走了進來。
「快跑啊！」城市老鼠大喊。
兩隻老鼠迅速地跑進牆邊的洞裡。
「唉，差一點。」城市老鼠說道：
「在這裡躲一下，再回去吃完我們的晚餐。」

但是鄉下老鼠很害怕，
他甚至嚇到說不出話來。
幾分鐘過去了。
「我們回去吃飯吧。」城市老鼠說。
「不了，謝謝你，我的朋友，」鄉下老鼠說道：
「我要回鄉下去了，我喜歡我簡樸的家，
雖然我家沒有很多食物，
但至少我可以平平靜靜地吃飯。再見了，我的朋友。」
鄉下老鼠就回自己的家去了。

Check Understanding 文意測驗

1 下列圖片中分別是什麼動物？
   a mouse 老鼠   b cat 貓

2 鄉下老鼠招待了什麼樣的食物？ a
   a 寒酸的食物   b 可口的食物   c 熱的食物

3 "plain" 是什麼意思？ b
   a 可口的   b 簡單的；簡樸的   c 小的

4 城市老鼠住在哪裡？ b
   a 一間小房子   b 一間大房子   c 一個公園

5 為什麼城市老鼠及鄉下老鼠要跑進洞裡？ b
   a 他們看見一隻狗走來。
   b 他們看見一隻貓走來。
   c 他們看見一些老鼠走來。

6 為什麼鄉下老鼠決定回家去？ c
   a 他不喜歡可口的食物。
   b 城市老鼠家裡沒有很多食物。
   c 他喜歡鄉下簡單但是平靜的生活。

● 回答問題

1 What did the country mouse serve to the city mouse? 鄉下老鼠準備了什麼食物招待城市老鼠？
   ⇨ He served some pieces of <u>corn</u>, green <u>peas</u>, and <u>berries</u>. 他準備了一些玉米、豌豆和莓子。

2 How did the country mouse feel about the cat? 鄉下老鼠對貓是什麼感覺？
   ⇨ He was very <u>frightened</u> of the cat. 他對貓感到非常害怕。

Vocabulary and Grammar Builder 字彙與文法練習

A 看圖填空：依照圖片選出正確的單字。

1 Dinner in the country was <u>plain</u>. 鄉下的晚餐很寒酸。

2 Dinner in the city was <u>delicious</u>. 城市的晚餐很可口。

3 There was a big <u>dining table</u>. 那是一張偌大的餐桌。

4 The country mouse was very <u>frightened</u>. 鄉下老鼠非常害怕。

B 過去式：圈出正確的單字，並填入空格中。

1 The country mouse ____served____ food to the city mouse. (serve) 鄉下老鼠為城市老鼠準備食物。
   serveed (served)

2 At last, they ____arrived____ at the city mouse's home. (arrive) 最後，他們到了城市老鼠的家。
   (arrived) arriveed

3 The two mice ____began____ to eat the dinner. (begin) 兩隻老鼠開始吃晚餐。
   beginned (began)

4 The country mouse ____went____ back to his home. (go) 鄉下老鼠回去自己的家。
   goed (went)

Counting to 100

數到 100

Reading Focus 閱讀焦點

- How high can you count? 你可以數到多大的數字呢？
- Can you count to 100 by tens? 你可以以十的倍數數到 100 嗎？
- Can you count backward? 你會倒著數數嗎？

Key Words 關鍵字彙

Counting by Tens 數十的倍數

10	20	30	40	50
ten 十	twenty 二十	thirty 三十	forty 四十	fifty 五十
60	70	80	90	100
sixty 六十	seventy 七十	eighty 八十	ninety 九十	one hundred 一百

Counting by Fives 數五的倍數

5	10	15	20	25
five 五	ten 十	fifteen 十五	twenty 二十	twenty-five 二十五
30	35	40	45	50
thirty 三十	thirty-five 三十五	forty 四十	forty-five 四十五	fifty 五十
55	60	65	70	75
fifty-five 五十五	sixty 六十	sixty-five 六十五	seventy 七十	seventy-five 七十五
80	85	90	95	100
eighty 八十	eighty-five 八十五	ninety 九十	ninety-five 九十五	one hundred 一百

Power Verbs 核心動詞

continue
延伸；繼續
Let's **continue** counting.
我們繼續數。

count by tens
以十的倍數數（數）
I can **count by tens**.
我能數十的倍數。

find out
找出
Let's **find out** the answer.
讓我們找出這個答案。

count by fives
以五的倍數數（數）
I can **count by fives**.
我能數五的倍數。

count backward
倒著數（數）
Let's **count backward**.
讓我們倒著數。

try
嘗試
Try counting backward from 20 to 10.
試著倒著數 20 到 10。

practice
練習
Practice counting out loud.
練習大聲數數。

be able to
可以
He **is able to** count backward.
他可以倒著數數。

Word Families 相關字彙

above
在……之後
What numbers are above 5?
在 5 之後是什麼數字？

between
在……之間
Say the numbers between 1 and 10.
說出 1 到 10 之間的數字。

Counting to 100　數到 100

你可以從 1 數到 20。
一、二、三、四、五、六、七、八、九、十、
十一、十二、十三、十四、十五、
十六、十七、十八、十九、二十。

那大一點的數字呢？
你可以數到 100 嗎？

首先，先讓我們從 20 數到 30。
接續在 20 之後的數字是：21、22、23、24、25、26、27、28、29、30。
二十一、二十二、二十三、二十四、二十五、二十六、二十七、二十八、二十九、三十。

現在，30 之後的數字有哪些呢？
讓我們數十的倍數，並找出答案。

十、二十、三十、四十、五十、
六十、七十、八十、九十、一百。

有時候我們可以數五的倍數，
讓我們用五的倍數數到 50。
五、十、十五、二十、二十五、
三十、三十五、四十、四十五、五十。

讓我們學習倒著數，
舉例來說，試著從 30 倒著數到 20，像這樣：
30、29、28、27、26、25、24、23、22、21、20。
繼續嘗試，你做得到的。

現在，讓我們大聲的練習從 1 數到 100。
你應該可以唸出 1 到 100 之間任何一個數字，
可以嗎？真棒！

3 Unit 10 Counting to 100

Check Understanding　文意測驗

1 下列圖片中分別是什麼？

 a counting **by fives** 數五的倍數 　　 **b** counting **backward** 倒著數

2 哪一組是十的倍數？ **a**

 a 10, 20, 30, 40, 50　　**b** 5, 10, 15, 20, 25　　**c** 1, 2, 3, 4, 5

3 哪一組是五的倍數？ **b**

 a 10, 20, 30, 40, 50　　**b** 5, 10, 15, 20, 25　　**c** 1, 2, 3, 4, 5

4 30, 29, 28, 27, 26 是＿＿＿＿數。 **c**

 a 以五的倍數　　**b** 往前　　**c** 倒著

● 回答問題

1 What are the numbers from 10 to 50 counting by tens? 用十的倍數數 1 到 50，有哪些數字？
 ⇨ They are <u>ten</u>, <u>twenty</u>, <u>thirty</u>, <u>forty</u>, and <u>fifty</u>. 有十、二十、三十、四十和五十。

2 What are the numbers from 60 to 100 counting by tens? 用十的倍數數 60 到 100，有哪些數字？
 ⇨ They are <u>sixty</u>, <u>seventy</u>, <u>eighty</u>, <u>ninety</u>, and <u>one</u> <u>hundred</u>. 有六十、七十、八十、九十、一百。

Vocabulary and Grammar Builder　字彙與文法練習

A 看圖填空：依照圖片選出正確的單字。

 1 Let's <u>continue</u> counting from 10 to 100. 讓我們從 10 數到 100。

 2 Let's count by <u>fives</u>. 讓我們數五的倍數。

 3 Let's <u>find out</u> the answer. 讓我們找出答案。

 4 Are you <u>able to</u> count backward? 你可以倒著數嗎？

B 介系詞：圈出正確的單字，並填入空格中。

 1 I can count ＿＿**by**＿＿ tens. 我會數十的倍數。
 　 (by) for

 2 He can count ＿＿**from**＿＿ 1 to 100. 他會從 1 數到 100。
 　 (from) in

 3 Say any number ＿＿**between**＿＿ 1 and 100. 說出任何 1 到 100 之間的數字。
 　 above (between)

 4 What numbers are ＿＿**above**＿＿ 30? 30 之後有些什麼數字？
 　 (above) between

125

What Do Artists Do?

藝術家都做些什麼？

Reading Focus 閱讀焦點

• What do artists make? 藝術家們創作什麼？

• What do artists need? 藝術家需要什麼？

• Who are some famous artists? 有哪些有名的藝術家？

Key Words 關鍵字彙

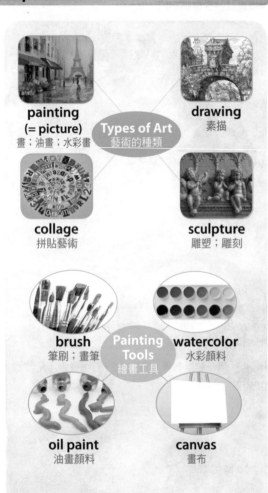

painting
(= picture)
畫；油畫；水彩畫

Types of Art
藝術的種類

drawing
素描

collage
拼貼藝術

sculpture
雕塑；雕刻

brush
筆刷；畫筆

Painting Tools
繪畫工具

watercolor
水彩顏料

oil paint
油畫顏料

canvas
畫布

Power Verbs 核心動詞

paint
繪畫；描繪

A painter **paints** pictures.
畫家畫圖。

sing
唱（歌）

A singer can **sing** well.
歌手可以把歌唱得很好。

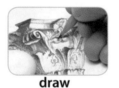

draw
繪畫；繪製

Some artists **draw** with pencils.
有些藝術家用鉛筆繪圖。

make
製作

Some artists **make** sculptures.
有些藝術家製作雕像。

Word Families: They Are All Artists 相關字彙：他們都是藝術家

painter
畫家

Artists
藝術家

singer
歌手

dancer
舞者

sculptor
雕刻家

What Do Artists Do? 藝術家都做些什麼？

藝術家就是創造藝術的人。
有些藝術家繪製圖畫，
有些藝術家用歌聲創造藝術，
其他藝術家設計建築和製作美麗的東西。

你喜歡畫畫嗎？
還是你喜歡堆積木？
那製作拼貼畫怎麼樣？
當你做這些事的時候，你都是在創造藝術。

有些藝術家用鉛筆在紙上作畫，
其他藝術家則是在畫布上作畫。

有些藝術家用畫筆和水彩作畫，
其他藝術家使用油畫顏料來作畫，
我們稱這些藝術家為畫家。

有些藝術家雕塑藝術品，
我們稱他們為雕刻家。

你知道哪些有名的藝術家嗎？
讓我們來看看世界上其中一幅最有名的畫作。

你以前曾經看過它嗎？
看看她的臉龐，
她快樂嗎？她正在看著你嗎？

這幅畫是由義大利藝術家李奧那多・達文西所繪製，
他在五百年前畫了這幅《蒙娜麗莎的微笑》，
這幅畫到現在還是受到人們的讚賞。

Check Understanding 文意測驗

1 下列圖片中分別是哪一種藝術品？

   a painting 繪畫   b sculpture 雕塑；雕刻

2 畫家會使用什麼？ c

   a 積木   b 黏土   c 筆刷；畫筆

3 《蒙娜麗莎的微笑》是什麼藝術品？ c

   a 雕塑   b 拼貼畫   c 繪畫

4 雕刻家製作_____。 a

   a 雕塑；雕刻   b 圖畫   c 歌曲

● 回答問題

1 Who are artists? 誰是藝術家？
   ⇨ Artists are people who make art. 藝術家就是創造藝術的人。

2 Who painted the *Mona Lisa*? 誰畫了《蒙娜麗莎的微笑》？
   ⇨ The Italian artist Leonardo da Vinci painted the *Mona Lisa*.
   義大利藝術家李奧那多・達文西畫了《蒙娜麗莎的微笑》。

Vocabulary and Grammar Builder 字彙與文法練習

Ⓐ 看圖填空：依照圖片選出正確的單字。

   1 Some painters paint pictures on a canvas. 有些畫家在畫布上作畫。

   2 Some artists sing. 有些藝術家唱歌。

   3 Some artists draw with pencils on paper. 有些藝術家用鉛筆在紙上作畫。

   4 A sculptor makes sculptures. 雕刻家雕塑藝術品。

Ⓑ 動名詞：圈出正確的單字，並填入空格中。

   1 When you draw a picture, you are ___making___ art. 當你畫圖的時候，你正在創造藝術。
      make (making)

   2 Is she ___looking___ at you? 她正在看著你嗎？
      look (looking)

   3 He is ___painting___ a picture on a canvas. 他在畫布上作畫。
      paint (painting)

   4 Sculptors ___make___ sculptures. 雕刻家雕塑藝術品。
      (make) making

Ballet Music

芭蕾舞曲

Reading Focus 閱讀焦點

- What is a ballet? 什麼是芭蕾？
- Who is a ballerina? 誰是芭蕾舞女演員？
- What are some famous ballets? 有哪些有名的芭蕾舞劇？

Key Words 關鍵字彙

Ballet
芭蕾

ballet dancer
芭蕾舞者

ballerina
芭蕾舞女演員

music
音樂

dance
舞蹈

The Nutcracker
《胡桃鉗》

Swan Lake
《天鵝湖》

The Nutcracker
《胡桃鉗》

nutcracker
胡桃鉗

Clara
克萊拉

prince
王子

kingdom
王國

Power Verbs 核心動詞

clap
拍（手）；鼓（掌）

Clap your hands.
拍手吧。

tap
輕點

Tap your toes.
用你的腳指輕點。

dance
跳舞

They **dance** very well.
他們舞跳得很好

love to
喜愛……

People **love to** dance.
人們喜歡跳舞。

tell a story
說故事

A ballet can **tell a story**.
芭蕾舞會說故事。

be performed
被表演

The ballet **is performed**
every year.
這場芭蕾每年都會表演。

come to life
活過來

A toy nutcracker
comes to life.
玩具胡桃鉗活過來了。

be composed
作曲

The Nutcracker
was composed
by Tchaikovsky.
《胡桃鉗》是柴可夫斯基作
的曲。

Ballet Music 芭蕾舞曲

當你聽到有趣、輕快的音樂，你會怎麼做？
你會拍手嗎？
還是你會輕點你的腳指？

有些音樂會讓你的身體擺動，
這就是舞蹈。
跳舞就是身體隨著音樂舞動，
很多人都喜歡跳舞，你呢？

舞蹈有非常多種類，
芭蕾是其中一種。
芭蕾不會唱歌、不會說話，
但是它可以透過音樂及舞蹈動作訴說故事。

《胡桃鉗》是其中一齣最有名的芭蕾舞劇，
它在每年的聖誕節都會表演。

這個故事是描述一個小女孩在聖誕節時所做的夢，
在夢中，玩具胡桃鉗活過來了，並且大戰鼠王。
然後，胡桃鉗變成了一位王子，
他帶著那位女孩——克萊拉——一起遊歷他的王國，
在那裡，他們看見了各式各樣的舞蹈。

《胡桃鉗》是柴可夫斯基作的曲，
柴可夫斯基是俄羅斯的作曲家，
他寫了很多有名的芭蕾舞劇，
像是《胡桃鉗》、《天鵝湖》和《睡美人》。

Check Understanding 文意測驗

1 下列圖片中分別是什麼？
   a ballet / ballet dancer 芭蕾 / 芭蕾舞者
   b *The Nutcracker* 《胡桃鉗》

2 什麼是舞蹈？ a
   a 跟著音樂擺動   b 唱歌   c 聽音樂

3 《胡桃鉗》是什麼？ b
   a 一位有名的作曲家   b 一齣有名的芭蕾舞劇   c 一個王國

4 芭蕾透過舞蹈_____訴說故事。 b
   a 歌曲   b 動作   c 聲音

● 回答問題

1 When is *The Nutcracker* performed? 《胡桃鉗》什麼時候表演？
   ⇨ It is performed <u>every</u> <u>year</u> around <u>Christmas</u>. 它每年都在聖誕節左右表演。

2 What ballets did Tchaikovsky write? 柴可夫斯基寫了哪些芭蕾舞劇？
   ⇨ He wrote *The Nutcracker*, *Swan Lake*, and *The Sleeping Beauty*.
     他寫了《胡桃鉗》、《天鵝湖》和《睡美人》。

Vocabulary and Grammar Builder 字彙與文法練習

A 看圖填空：依照圖片選出正確的單字。

1 People love to <u>dance</u>. 人們喜歡跳舞。
2 Tchaikovsky was a Russian <u>composer</u>. 柴可夫斯基是俄羅斯的作曲家。
3 Tchaikovsky wrote many famous <u>ballets</u>. 柴可夫斯基寫了很多有名的芭蕾舞劇。
4 The <u>nutcracker</u> fights the Mouse King. 胡桃鉗大戰鼠王。

B 被動式：圈出正確的單字，並填入空格中。

1 *The Nutcracker* is _____performed_____ every year. 《胡桃鉗》每年都會表演。
   perform (performed)
2 They _____perform_____ *The Nutcracker* every year. 他們每年都會表演《胡桃鉗》。
   (perform) are performed
3 *The Nutcracker* was _____composed_____ by Tchaikovsky. 《胡桃鉗》是柴可夫斯基作的曲。
   compose (composed)
4 Tchaikovsky _____composed_____ *The Nutcracker*. 柴可夫斯基寫了《胡桃鉗》。
   (composed) was composed

129

A 看圖填空：依照圖片選出正確的單字。

1 Edison <u>invented</u> the light bulb.　愛迪生發明燈泡。

2 <u>Astronauts</u> wear spacesuits.　太空人穿著太空衣。

3 A <u>thunderstorm</u> has thunder and lightning.　大雷雨挾帶打雷和閃電。

4 A hurricane <u>forms</u> on the ocean.　颶風在海面上形成。

B 圈出正確的單字，並填入空格中。

1 Thomas Edison was very _____curious_____.　湯瑪士‧愛迪生很有好奇心。
　　　　　　　　　　　　curious　convenient

2 Space shuttles lift __off__ from the Kennedy Space Center.　太空梭從甘迺迪太空中心發射。
　　　　　　　　　on　off

3 Storms can ___bring___ heavy rain.　風暴會帶來大雨。
　　　　　　　strike　bring

4 The hurricane ___destroyed___ the city.　颶風摧毀城市。
　　　　　　　lifted　destroyed

C 選出正確的單字，並填入空格中。

1 Thomas Edison was <u>born</u> in 1847 in America.　湯瑪士‧愛迪生於 1847 年出生在美國。

2 When Edison grew up, he became an <u>inventor</u>.　當愛迪生長大後，他變成一位發明家。

3 Thanks to <u>electric lights</u>, we can see at night.　感謝有電燈，讓我們能在黑夜中看見東西。

4 <u>Inventions</u> make our work easier and faster.　發明使我們的工作更簡單、更有效率。

5 Astronauts <u>explore</u> space and learn about it.　太空人探索宇宙並且獲悉相關的知識。

6 Who was the first <u>human</u> in space?　誰是第一位進入太空的人？

7 Many astronauts go into space from the Kennedy <u>Space Center</u>.
　　很多太空人都是從甘迺迪太空中心進入宇宙的。

8 Space <u>shuttles</u> lift off from the center.　太空梭從太空中心發射。

D 選出正確的單字，並填入空格中。

1 Flash! <u>Lightning</u> strikes across the sky.　稍縱即逝的閃光，閃電劃破天空。

2 Boom! <u>Thunder</u> makes a loud sound.　轟隆！雷發出巨大的隆隆聲。

3 Sometimes heavy rain causes <u>floods</u>.　有時候豪雨會造成水災。

4 Storms can be <u>harmful</u>.　風暴是有傷害性的。

5 Big <u>thunderstorms</u> can make a tornado.　巨大的雷雨會變成龍捲風。

6 A tornado has a <u>funnel-shaped</u> cloud with strong winds.
　　龍捲風是漏斗狀的雲，夾帶強勁的風勢。

7 A tornado can <u>destroy</u> buildings and kill people.　龍捲風會摧毀房屋，奪走人命。

8 A hurricane <u>forms</u> on the ocean.　颶風在海洋上形成。

A 看圖填空：依照圖片選出正確的單字。

1 Most plants grow from <u>seeds</u>. 大部分的植物都是由種子開始成長。

2 Snakes <u>slither</u> on the ground. 蛇在地上爬行。

3 The <u>caterpillar</u> builds a cocoon. 毛毛蟲會建造出一個蛹。

4 Birds have feathers in <u>common</u>. 鳥兒都有羽毛。

B 圈出正確的單字，並填入空格中。

1 First, he ___<u>digs</u>___ holes in the ground. 首先，他在地上挖了幾個洞。
   dig (digs)

2 Some snakes are ___<u>poisonous</u>___. 有些蛇是有毒的。
   poison (poisonous)

3 A butterfly's eyes are ___<u>on</u>___ its head. 蝴蝶的眼睛在頭上。
   at (on)

4 A caterpillar changes ___<u>inside</u>___ its cocoon. 毛毛蟲在蛹中蛻變。
   (inside) outside

C 選出正確的單字，並填入空格中。

1 Johnny is going to <u>plant</u> some seeds in his garden. 強尼要把這些種子種在花園裡。

2 First, roots <u>grow down</u> into the soil. 一開始，根向下紮進泥土裡。

3 Next, stems <u>grow up</u>. 接著，莖長出來了。

4 Then, leaves and <u>flowers</u> begin to grow. 然後，葉子和花開始生長。

5 Snakes have no arms, legs, or <u>wings</u>. 蛇沒有手臂、腳或是翅膀。

6 Snakes move their bodies <u>back and forth</u>. 蛇來來回回扭動牠們的身體。

7 Snakes <u>molt</u> at least once a year. 蛇一年至少脫一次皮。

8 <u>Poisonous</u> snakes use poison to kill other animals. 毒蛇用毒液獵殺其他動物。

D 選出正確的單字，並填入空格中。

1 Butterflies cannot fly from <u>birth</u>. 蝴蝶不是一出生就會飛。

2 A butterfly begins in an <u>egg</u>. 蝴蝶一開始只是一顆卵。

3 Then, a <u>caterpillar</u> comes out of the egg. 然後，卵孵出了毛毛蟲。

4 Inside the <u>cocoon</u>, the caterpillar changes. 在蛹中，毛毛蟲蛻變了。

5 Birds have feathers <u>in common</u>. 鳥兒都有羽毛。

6 Birds lay eggs in <u>nests</u>. 鳥兒在巢裡孵蛋。

7 Later, the eggs <u>hatch</u>, and baby birds are born. 之後，蛋會孵化，幼鳥就出生了。

8 Parent birds <u>feed</u> their baby birds. 親鳥餵養牠們的幼鳥。

A 看圖填空：依照圖片選出正確的單字。

1 The country mouse was very <u>frightened</u>. 鄉下老鼠很害怕。

2 Let's count by <u>tens</u>. 讓我們數十的倍數。

3 Leonardo da Vinci <u>painted</u> the *Mona Lisa*. 李奧那多 · 達文西畫了《蒙娜麗莎的微笑》。

4 A <u>ballet</u> can tell a story. 芭蕾舞可以訴說故事。

B 圈出正確的單字，並填入空格中。

1 The country mouse ___went___ back to his home. 鄉下老鼠回去自己家。
   goed (went)

2 Say any number ___between___ 1 and 100. 說出任何 1 到 100 之間的數字。
   above (between)

3 Artists are people who ___make___ art. 藝術家是創作藝術的人。
   (make) making

4 The ballet is ___performed___ every year. 這場芭蕾舞劇每年都會表演。
   (performed) perform

C 選出正確的單字，並填入空格中。

1 Once upon a time, there were two <u>mice</u>. 很久很久以前，有兩隻老鼠。

2 At last, they <u>arrived</u> at the city mouse's home. 最後，他們到了城市老鼠的家。

3 He invited his friend into a large <u>kitchen</u>. 他邀請他的朋友進到一間很大的廚房。

4 On the huge <u>dining</u> table, there was a lot of delicious food.
   在偌大的餐桌上，擺滿了好多可口的食物。

5 Let's <u>continue</u> counting from 20 to 30. 讓我們繼續從 20 數到 30。

6 Let's count <u>backward</u> from 30 to 20. 讓我們從 30 倒著數到 20。

7 Now, let's practice counting <u>out loud</u> from 1 to 100. 現在，大聲練習從 1 數到 100。

8 You should be <u>able to</u> say the name of any number between 1 and 100.
   你應該可以唸出 1 到 100 之間任何一個數字。

D 選出正確的單字，並填入空格中。

1 <u>Artists</u> are people who make art. 藝術家就是創造藝術的人。

2 Some artists paint pictures on a <u>canvas</u>. 有些藝術家在畫布上作畫。

3 Some artists use brushes and <u>watercolors</u>. 有些藝術家使用畫筆和水彩。

4 The *Mona Lisa* is a <u>painting</u> by Leonardo da Vinci.
   《蒙娜麗莎的微笑》是李奧那多 · 達文西畫的。

5 <u>Dancing</u> is moving to music. 跳舞就是隨著音樂擺動。

6 *The Nutcracker* is one of the most famous <u>ballets</u>. 《胡桃鉗》是其中一齣最有名的芭蕾舞劇。

7 In a dream, a toy nutcracker <u>comes to life</u> and fights a Mouse King.
   在夢中，玩具胡桃鉗活過來了，並且大戰鼠王。

8 *The Nutcracker* was <u>composed</u> by Tchaikovsky. 《胡桃鉗》是柴可夫斯基作的曲。

Authors

Michael A. Putlack

Michael A. Putlack graduated from Tufts University in Medford, Massachusetts, USA, where he got his B.A. in History and English and his M.A. in History. He has written a number of books for children, teenagers, and adults.

e-Creative Contents

A creative group that develops English contents and products for ESL and EFL students.

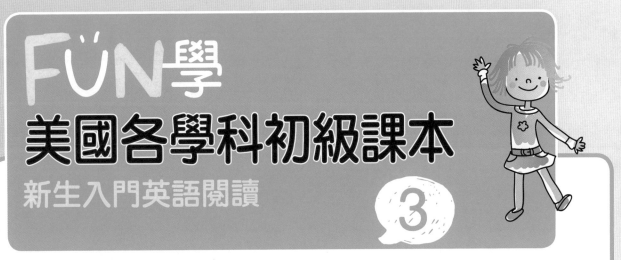

作　者　Michael A. Putlack & e-Creative Contents

譯　者　陸葵珍

編　輯　賴祖兒／陸葵珍

主　編　丁宥暄

內文排版　謝青秀／林書玉

封面設計　林書玉

製程管理　洪巧玲

發 行 人　黃朝萍

出 版 者　寂天文化事業股份有限公司

電　話　+886-(0)2-2365-9739

傳　真　+886-(0)2-2365-9835

網　址　www.icosmos.com.tw

讀者服務　onlineservice@icosmos.com.tw

出版日期　2023 年 9 月 二版再刷（寂天雲隨身聽 APP 版）(0202)

國家圖書館出版品預行編目資料

Fun學美國各學科初級課本 3：新生入門英語閱讀 (寂天雲隨身聽APP版) = American textbook reading key/ Michael A. Putlack, e-Creative Contents著. --
二版. -- [臺北市]: 寂天文化, 2021.09-
　冊；　公分
ISBN 978-626-300-052-0 (第3冊：菊8K平裝).

1.英語 2.讀本

805.18　　　　　　　　　　　110013028

FÜN學
美國各學科初級課本
新生入門英語閱讀 二版

3

AMERiCAN
SCHOOL
TEXTBOOK

Reading
Key BASIC

WORKBOOK
練習本

Thanks, Thomas Edison

A Write the meaning of each word and phrase in Chinese.

1	Thomas Edison _____	19	invent _____
2	turn on _____	20	electric light bulb _____
3	light _____	21	thanks to _____
4	dark _____	22	at night _____
5	electric light _____	23	phonograph _____
6	famous _____	24	listen to music _____
7	inventor _____	25	stereo _____
8	be born _____	26	motion picture camera _____
9	America _____	27	see a movie _____
10	curious _____	28	more than _____
11	always _____	29	life _____
12	ask a question _____	30	convenient _____
13	Why? _____	31	more convenient _____
14	Why is that? _____	32	in the world _____
15	grow up _____	33	work _____
16	become _____	34	easier _____
17	call _____	35	faster _____
18	invention _____	36	some of _____

B Choose the word that best completes each sentence.

curious	inventions	electric lights	convenient

1 Thomas Edison was a _____ boy.

2 Thomas Edison made many _____ .

3 Thanks to _____, we can see at night.

4 His inventions made our lives more _____ .

▶ B, C大題解答請參照主冊課文
A大題解答請參照Word List（主冊P. 93）

3

Listen to the passage and fill in the blanks. 25

We turn on a _____ when it's dark.

Do you know who made the _____ light?

It was Thomas _____.

Thomas Edison was a _____ inventor.

He was _____ in 1847 in America.

He was a very _____ boy.

He always _____ questions. "Why?" "Why is that?"

When he _____, he became an inventor.

An _____ makes new things.

We call these new things _____.

Thomas Edison _____ many inventions.

He invented the electric light _____.

_____ to electric lights, we can see at night.

He invented the _____.

Thanks to him, we can _____ _____ music with a stereo.

He invented the _____ picture camera.

Thanks to him, we can see _____.

Thomas Edison also _____ many other things.

He made more than _____ inventions!

His inventions made our lives more _____.

There are many _____ inventions in the world.

Inventions make our work easier and _____.

Do you know _____ of them?

The First Man Into Space

A Write the meaning of each word and phrase in Chinese.

1	space	_____	20 Florida	_____
2	like	_____	21 USA	_____
3	like V-ing	_____	22 space shuttle	_____
4	like to V	_____	23 lift off	_____
5	travel	_____	24 wear	_____
6	new place	_____	25 spacesuit	_____
7	would like to	_____	26 protect	_____
8	How about V-ing?	_____	27 American	_____
9	travel into	_____	28 moon	_____
10	astronaut	_____	29 Neil Armstrong	_____
11	explore	_____	30 walk on	_____
12	learn about	_____	31 Sally Ride	_____
13	the first	_____	32 woman	_____
14	human	_____	33 Mae Jemison	_____
15	Yuri Gagarin	_____	34 African-American	_____
16	Russian	_____	35 Dennis Tito	_____
17	go into	_____	36 space tourist	_____
18	for the first time	_____	37 travel around	_____
19	Kennedy Space Center	_____	38 Earth	_____

B Choose the word that best completes each sentence.

moon	explore	human	astronauts

1 Astronauts _____ space and learn about it.

2 Who was the first _____ in space?

3 _____ wear spacesuits.

4 Neil Armstrong was the first person to walk on the _____.

5

Listen to the passage and fill in the blanks. 26

Do you like _____ to new places?

Where _____ you like to go?

How about traveling into _____?

Some _____ travel into space.

They are _____.

Astronauts _____ space and learn about it.

Who was the _____ human in space?

It was Yuri Gagarin, a _____ astronaut.

He went into space for the first time in _____.

This is the Kennedy Space _____.

It is in _____ in the USA.

Many astronauts go into space from the _____ Space Center.

Space shuttles _____ _____ from the center.

Astronauts wear _____.

Their spacesuits _____ them in space.

In 1969, _____ astronauts went to the moon for the first time.

Neil Armstrong was the first person to _____ on the moon.

Sally Ride was the first American _____ in space.

Mae Jemison was the first _____-American woman in space.

Dennis Tito was the first space _____.

He traveled around _____ in 2001.

A **Write the meaning of each word and phrase in Chinese.**

1 storm _____
2 look up at _____
3 sky _____
4 cloud _____
5 dark _____
6 come _____
7 flash _____
8 lightning _____
9 strike _____
10 across _____
11 boom _____
12 thunder _____
13 make a sound _____
14 loud _____
15 thunderstorm _____
16 sometimes _____
17 harmful _____

18 bring _____
19 strong wind _____
20 heavy rain _____
21 heavy snow _____
22 cause _____
23 flood(s) _____
24 stream _____
25 overflow _____
26 be covered with _____
27 may _____
28 fall _____
29 snowstorm _____
30 be called _____
31 blizzard _____
32 heavily _____
33 so...that... _____
34 white _____

B **Choose the word that best completes each sentence.**

thunder	floods	harmful	strikes

1 _____ makes a loud sound.

2 Lightning _____ across the sky.

3 Storms can be _____.

4 Sometimes heavy rain causes _____.

C **Listen to the passage and fill in the blanks.** 27

Look up at the _____.

The _____ are big and dark.

A storm is _____.

Flash! Lightning _____ across the sky.

Boom! Thunder makes a _____ sound.

It is a _____.

Sometimes we have _____.

Storms can be _____.

Storms can bring strong _____.

Storms can _____ heavy rain or snow.

A thunderstorm has thunder, lightning, and _____ rain.

Sometimes lightning strikes trees and tall _____.

Sometimes heavy rain _____ floods.

Rivers and streams _____.

Some land is _____ with water.

When it is cold, a lot of snow may _____.

A big _____ is called a blizzard.

A _____ has strong winds.

In a blizzard, snow falls so _____ that people can only see white.

Tornadoes and Hurricanes

A Write the meaning of each word and phrase in Chinese.

1	tornado	_____	22 fast	_____
2	hurricane	_____	23 can be	_____
3	begin to	_____	24 dangerous	_____
4	look strange	_____	25 lift	_____
5	cloud	_____	26 even	_____
6	low	_____	27 truck	_____
7	purple	_____	28 blow away	_____
8	blow	_____	29 destroy	_____
9	hard	_____	30 building	_____
10	suddenly	_____	31 kill	_____
11	loud	_____	32 huge	_____
12	alarm	_____	33 rainstorm	_____
13	sound	_____	34 be called	_____
14	rush to	_____	35 form	_____
15	shelter	_____	36 on the ocean	_____
16	be coming	_____	37 move onto	_____
17	thunderstorm	_____	38 land	_____
18	funnel-shaped	_____	39 fall	_____
19	spin	_____	40 during	_____
20	like	_____	41 center	_____
21	top	_____	42 the eye	_____

B Choose the word that best completes each sentence.

funnel-shaped	tornado	hurricane	shelter

1 Big thunderstorms can make a _____.

2 A tornado has a _____ cloud with strong winds.

3 People rush to _____.

4 The center of a _____ is called the eye.

C **Listen to the passage and fill in the blanks.** 28

The sky begins to look _____.

The clouds are low and _____.

The wind begins to _____ hard.

Suddenly, a loud _____ sounds.

People rush to _____.

A _____ is coming.

Big _____ can make a tornado.

It has a _____-shaped cloud with strong winds.

This funnel-shaped cloud _____ like a top.

Tornado _____ blow very fast.

A tornado can be very _____.

A tornado can _____ many things.

It can even lift _____ and blow them away.

It can _____ buildings and kill people.

A huge rainstorm is called a _____.

A hurricane has very _____ winds.

It _____ on the ocean.

But hurricanes often _____ onto land.

Heavy rain falls _____ a hurricane.

The center of a hurricane is called the _____.

How Do Plants Grow?

A Write the meaning of each word and phrase in Chinese.

1 plant _____
2 grow _____
3 most _____
4 seed _____
5 these _____
6 picture _____
7 sunflower _____
8 pea _____
9 bell pepper _____
10 strawberry _____
11 look different _____
12 grow into _____
13 bean _____
14 be going to _____
15 garden _____
16 first _____
17 dig _____
18 hole _____
19 ground _____

20 put _____
21 then _____
22 cover _____
23 with soil _____
24 need _____
25 water _____
26 every day _____
27 slowly _____
28 start to _____
29 root _____
30 grow down _____
31 next _____
32 stem _____
33 grow up _____
34 last _____
35 make fruits _____
36 later _____
37 become _____

B Choose the word that best completes each sentence.

seeds	fruits	digs	soil

1 _____ grow into new plants.

2 First, he _____ holes in the ground.

3 Then, he covers the holes with _____.

4 Flowers make _____.

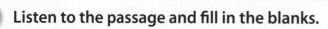

C **Listen to the passage and fill in the blanks.** 29

Most plants grow from _____.

What are the seeds in these _____?

    sunflower   _____   bell pepper   strawberry

Seeds look different, but they grow into new _____.

Johnny has some _____ seeds.

He is going to _____ them in his garden.

First, he _____ holes in the ground.

He _____ the seeds in the holes.

Then, he _____ the holes with soil.

Seeds need _____ to grow.

They also need _____.

So Johnny _____ the seeds every day.

Slowly, the seeds _____ to grow.

First, roots grow _____ into the soil.

Next, _____ grow up.

Then, _____ and flowers begin to grow.

Last, the flowers make _____.

These fruits have _____.

Later, these seeds grow and _____ new plants.

A World of Animals: Snakes

A Write the meaning of each word and phrase in Chinese.

1 snake _____

2 look at _____

3 anaconda _____

4 cobra _____

5 boa _____

6 rattlesnake _____

7 special _____

8 arm _____

9 leg _____

10 wing _____

11 walk _____

12 run _____

13 move _____

14 slither _____

15 back and forth _____

16 let _____

17 in all directions _____

18 lay eggs _____

19 hatch _____

20 at one time _____

21 molt _____

22 at least _____

23 once a year _____

24 skin _____

25 tongue _____

26 sense _____

27 fang _____

28 bite _____

29 poisonous _____

30 poison _____

31 kill _____

32 dangerous _____

33 harmful _____

34 human _____

B Choose the word that best completes each sentence.

molt	slither	hatch	poisonous

1 Snakes _____ on the ground.

2 More than 40 eggs _____ at one time.

3 Snakes _____ at least once a year.

4 _____ snakes use poison to kill other animals.

Listen to the passage and fill in the blanks. 30

Look at the _____.

What are _____ animals?

anaconda _____ boa rattlesnake

They are all _____.

Snakes are _____.

They have no arms, legs, or _____.

They can't _____ or run.

So _____ do they move?

They _____ on the ground.

Snakes move their bodies back and _____.

This lets them move in all _____.

Most snakes lay _____.

More than 40 eggs _____ at one time.

Also, snakes _____ at least once a year.

Then, new skin _____.

Snakes have long _____, too.

They use their tongues to _____ other animals.

And most snakes have long _____.

They _____ with their fangs.

Some snakes are _____.

Poisonous snakes use _____ to kill other animals.

They are very _____.

But most snakes are not _____ to humans.

Amazing Changes: Butterflies

A Write the meaning of each word and phrase in Chinese.

1 amazing _____

2 butterfly _____

3 every year _____

4 nearly _____

5 type _____

6 take a close look at _____

7 body part _____

8 head _____

9 thorax _____

10 abdomen _____

11 antenna _____

12 be used for _____

13 touching _____

14 smelling _____

15 wing _____

16 fly _____

17 forewing _____

18 hind wing _____

19 from birth _____

20 change _____

21 over time _____

22 caterpillar _____

23 come out of _____

24 grow bigger _____

25 build _____

26 cocoon _____

27 hard _____

28 covering _____

29 inside _____

30 a week _____

31 adult _____

B Choose the word that best completes each sentence.

caterpillar	butterfly	cocoon	wings

1 A _____ has three body parts.

2 A butterfly has four _____ .

3 A _____ comes out of the egg.

4 After about a week, a butterfly comes out of the _____ .

Every year, we can see many _____.
There are _____ 20,000 types of butterflies.

Let's _____ a close look at a butterfly.
A butterfly has three body _____.
It has a head, a thorax, and an _____.

A butterfly's eyes are on its _____.
It _____ with its eyes.
A butterfly's _____ are also on its head.
Antennas are used for _____ touching and smelling.

A butterfly has six _____.
They are on _____ thorax.
A butterfly's wings are also on its _____.
It _____ with its wings.
A butterfly has four wings: two _____ and two hind wings.

Butterflies cannot fly from _____.
They _____ over time.
A butterfly _____ in an egg.
Then, a caterpillar _____ out of the egg.

The caterpillar eats leaves and grows _____.
Then, it builds a _____.
This is a hard _____.
Inside the cocoon, the _____ changes.
After about a _____, a butterfly comes out of the cocoon.
Now, it's an _____ butterfly.

Birds Are Animals

A Write the meaning of each word and phrase in Chinese.

1 bird _____

2 eagle _____

3 chicken _____

4 duck _____

5 peacock _____

6 have in common _____

7 different _____

8 kind _____

9 feather _____

10 cover _____

11 body _____

12 beak _____

13 mouth _____

14 peck at _____

15 nest _____

16 sit on _____

17 keep...warm _____

18 hatch _____

19 be born _____

20 parent bird _____

21 feed _____

22 ostrich _____

23 huge _____

24 kiwi _____

25 either _____

B Choose the word that best completes each sentence.

| peck | feathers | nests | keep | fly | either |

1 _____ cover birds' body.

2 Birds lay eggs in _____.

3 Birds sit on their eggs to _____ them warm.

4 Birds _____ at food with their beaks.

5 Ostriches are huge birds, but they cannot _____.

6 Kiwis cannot fly _____.

Listen to the passage and fill in the blanks. 32

Look at the _____.

    eagle   chicken   _____   peacock

What do they have in _____?
They are all _____.
Birds are _____.
There are many different _____ of birds.

Birds have _____.
These _____ their bodies.

Birds also have _____.
Most birds use their wings to _____.

Birds have _____, too.
These are their _____.
Birds _____ at food with their beaks.

Birds lay eggs in _____.
_____ birds sit on their eggs.
This _____ their eggs warm.
Later, the eggs hatch, and _____ birds are born.
When birds _____, they cannot fly.
Parent birds _____ them.

Some birds are very _____.
Ostriches are _____ birds.
They cannot fly, but they can run very _____.
Kiwis cannot fly _____.

09 The City Mouse and the Country Mouse

A **Write the meaning of each word and phrase in Chinese.**

1	city _____	32	at last _____
2	mouse _____	33	arrive at _____
3	country _____	34	must be _____
4	once upon a time _____	35	hungry _____
5	mice _____	36	have dinner _____
6	friend _____	37	invite _____
7	one _____	38	kitchen _____
8	live in _____	39	Help yourself. _____
9	in the country _____	40	enough _____
10	the other _____	41	dining table _____
11	in the city _____	42	a lot of _____
12	one day _____	43	lots of _____
13	go to visit _____	44	bread _____
14	set the table _____	45	cheese _____
15	dinner _____	46	meat _____
16	serve _____	47	potato _____
17	some pieces of _____	48	fruit _____
18	corn _____	49	cake _____
19	green pea _____	50	just then _____
20	berry _____	51	cat _____
21	look around _____	52	run _____
22	plain _____	53	shout _____
23	what _____	54	quickly _____
24	what we eat _____	55	through _____
25	come with me _____	56	hole _____
26	delicious _____	57	wall _____
27	once _____	58	That was close. _____
28	taste _____	59	wait _____
29	wonderful _____	60	for a while _____
30	return _____	61	finish _____
31	for a long time _____	62	frightened _____

63 even	_____	67 No, thank you. _____
64 a few minutes	_____	68 simple _____
65 pass	_____	69 in peace _____
66 go back	_____	70 goodbye _____

B **Choose the word that best completes each sentence.**

went back	mice	hole	close
dining table	frightened	kitchen	

1 Once upon a time, there were two _____.

2 On the huge _____, there was a lot of delicious food.

3 He invited his friend into a large _____.

4 The two mice quickly ran through a small _____ in the wall.

5 "Whew! That was _____," said the city mouse.

6 The country mouse was very _____.

7 The country mouse _____ to his home.

20

Listen to the passage and fill in the blanks.

Once upon a time, there were two _____.
They were _____.
One _____ lived in a small house in the country.
The other mouse _____ in a large house in the city.

One day, the city mouse went to _____ his friend in the country.
The _____ mouse was so happy to see the city mouse.
He set the table for _____.
He _____ some pieces of corn, green peas, and berries.

The city mouse _____ around the table and said,
"Oh, my! This is all you have? Is this _____ dinner?
How can you eat such _____ food every day, my friend?"
"I'm sorry," _____ the country mouse.
"But this is what we eat in the country _____ day," he said.

"Come _____ me to the city," said the city mouse.
"What is in the city?" _____ the country mouse.
"There is a lot of _____ food," answered the city mouse.
"Once you have _____ all the wonderful food,
you will never want to _____ to the country."

So the two mice _____ to the city.
The mice _____ for a long time.
At last, they _____ at the city mouse's home.
He lived in a _____ big house.
"You must be _____. We will have dinner _____," said
the city mouse.
He invited his friend into a large _____.
"Help yourself. There is _____ food for us," said the city mouse.

On the huge _____ table, there was a lot of delicious food.

There were lots of bread and _____.

There were lots of meat and _____.

There were fruits and _____, too.

"See," _____ the city mouse.

"This is _____ we eat in the city every day."

"You were _____, my friend. This is a very good dinner,"

answered the country _____.

The two mice _____ to eat the dinner.

Just then, the door _____, and they saw a cat coming.

"Run!" _____ the city mouse.

The two mice quickly _____ through a small hole in the wall.

"Whew! That was _____," said the city mouse.

"Just wait here for a _____, and then we can finish our dinner."

But the county mouse was very _____.

He could not _____ talk.

A few _____ passed.

"Let's go _____ and eat," said the city mouse.

"No, _____ you, my friend," said the country mouse.

"I'm _____ back to the country. I like my _____ house.

There is not much _____ at my house.

But I can eat it in _____. Goodbye, my friend."

The country mouse _____ back to his home.

22

A Write the meaning of each word and phrase in Chinese.

1 counting _____

2 count _____

3 from...to... _____

4 What about...? _____

5 bigger number _____

6 continue _____

7 above _____

8 count by tens _____

9 find out _____

10 count by fives _____

11 count backward _____

12 for example _____

13 try _____

14 go ahead _____

15 go ahead and try _____

16 practice _____

17 out loud _____

18 be able to _____

19 any number _____

20 between _____

21 Good job! _____

B Choose the word that best completes each sentence.

fives	able	backward	practice

1 Sometimes people count by _____.

2 Let's learn to count _____.

3 Now, let's _____ counting out loud from 1 to 100.

4 You should be _____ to say the name of any number between 1 and 100.

Listen to the passage and fill in the blanks.

You can _____ from 1 to 20.
One, two, three, four, five, six, seven, _____, nine, ten.
Eleven, _____, thirteen, fourteen, fifteen.
Sixteen, seventeen, eighteen, nineteen, _____.

What about bigger _____?
Can you count to _____?

First, _____ count from 20 to 30.
After 20, the numbers _____: 21, 22, 23, 24, 25, 26, 27, 28, 29, 30.
Twenty-one, twenty-two, twenty-three, _____, twenty-five.
Twenty-six, twenty-seven, twenty-eight, twenty-nine, _____.

Now, what numbers are _____ 30?
Let's count by _____ and find out.
Ten, twenty, thirty, forty, _____.
Sixty, seventy, eighty, ninety, one _____.
Sometimes _____ count by fives, too.
Let's count by _____ to 50.
Five, ten, _____, twenty, twenty-five.
Thirty, thirty-five, forty, _____, fifty.

Let's learn to count _____.
For _____, try counting backward from 30 to 20 like this:
30, 29, 28, 27, 26, 25, 24, 23, 22, 21, 20.
Go _____ and try. You can do it.

Now, let's practice counting _____ _____ from 1 to 100.
You should be _____ _____ say the name of any number
between 1 and 100.
Can you? Good _____!

What Do Artists Do?

A Write the meaning of each word and phrase in Chinese.

1 artist _____
2 art _____
3 make art _____
4 paint _____
5 sing _____
6 build _____
7 draw _____
8 draw a picture _____
9 block _____
10 build with blocks _____
11 collage _____
12 pencil _____
13 on paper _____
14 paint a picture _____
15 on a canvas _____
16 brush _____
17 watercolor _____

18 oil paint _____
19 painter _____
20 sculpture _____
21 sculptor _____
22 famous _____
23 one of... _____
24 the most famous _____
25 painting _____
26 Have you ever...? _____
27 look at _____
28 Italian _____
29 Leonardo da Vinci _____
30 the *Mona Lisa* _____
31 around _____
32 still _____
33 enjoy V-ing _____
34 picture _____

B Choose the word that best completes each sentence.

paint	artists	watercolors	sculptors

1 _____ are people who make art.

2 Some artists use brushes and _____.

3 Other artists use oil paints to _____ pictures.

4 _____ make sculptures.

C   **Listen to the passage and fill in the blanks.**   35

Artists are people _____ make art.

Some _____ paint.

Some artists _____.

Others build _____ and make beautiful things.

Do you like to _____ pictures?

Or do you like to build with _____?

How about making _____?

When you do these things, you are _____ art.

Some artists draw with _____ on paper.

Other artists paint pictures on a _____.

Some artists use _____ and watercolors.

Other artists use oil _____ to paint pictures.

We call them _____.

Some artists make _____.

We call them _____.

Do you know any _____ painters?

Let's see one of the most famous _____ in the world.

Have you _____ seen it before?

Look at her _____.

Is she happy? Is she _____ at you?

It is a painting by the _____ artist Leonardo da Vinci.

He _____ the *Mona Lisa* around 500 years ago.

But people still _____ looking at the picture.

26

A Write the meaning of each word and phrase in Chinese.

1 ballet _____
2 fun _____
3 clap _____
4 tap _____
5 toe _____
6 move _____
7 dancing _____
8 love to _____
9 dance _____
10 many kinds of _____
11 dance _____
12 tell a story _____
13 movement _____
14 dancer _____
15 *The Nutcracker* _____
16 perform _____
17 be performed _____
18 every year _____
19 Christmas _____
20 young _____

21 girl _____
22 dream _____
23 toy _____
24 nutcracker _____
25 come to life _____
26 fight _____
27 Mouse King _____
28 become _____
29 prince _____
30 Clara _____
31 travel to _____
32 kingdom _____
33 watch _____
34 compose _____
35 be composed by _____
36 Tchaikovsky _____
37 Russian _____
38 composer _____
39 *Swan Lake* _____
40 *The Sleeping Beauty* _____

B Choose the word that best completes each sentence.

composed	dancing	ballet	famous

1 _____ is moving to music.

2 A _____ has no singing or talking.

3 *The Nutcracker* is one of the most _____ ballets.

4 *The Nutcracker* was _____ by Tchaikovsky.

C **Listen to the passage and fill in the blanks.** 36

What do you do when you hear a _____, happy song?
Do you _____ your hands?
Do you _____ your toes?

Sometimes music can _____ you move.
That is _____.
Dancing is _____ to music.
Many people _____ to dance. Do you?

There are many kinds of _____.
Ballet is one _____.
A ballet has no _____ or talking.
But it can tell a story by the _____ of dancers and music.

The Nutcracker is one of the _____ famous ballets.
It is performed every year _____ Christmas.

It tells the story of a young girl's _____ on Christmas.
In a dream, a toy _____ comes to life and fights a Mouse King.
Then, the nutcracker becomes a _____.
He and the girl—Clara—travel to his _____.
There, they _____ all kinds of dancing.

The Nutcracker was composed _____ Tchaikovsky.
Tchaikovsky was a _____ composer.
He _____ many famous ballets.
He wrote *The Nutcracker*, *Swan Lake*, and *The Sleeping* _____.